10621597

High praise for writing by Max Yoho

WITH THE WISDOM OF OWLS

"The first sentence in the book is, 'Never let reality limit your life.' And this book stands as a testimony that Max Yoho practices what he preaches. The fun I had reading it proves I have elbowed reality into its proper place in my life. If reality is disrupting your happiness, this book is your chance to take your stand."

—**Dalton Roberts**, *Chattannooga Times Free Press*

Anything Max Yoho writes is worth reading so you must not miss this slim, new volume. Every page offers something unique, humorous and different and, as with Max's other works, the reader will benefit from reading it more than once."

—**Bill Shaffer**, Producer/Director, KTWU-TV, Channel 11

THE REVIVAL

"Yoho's book is...my kind of lunacy!"

—**Baxter Black**, Cowboy, Poet, and Humorist

"I embarrassed myself laughing"

—**Jeff Veteto**, Houston, Texas

THE MOON BUTTER ROUTE

"2006 Kansas Notable Book"   —Kansas Center for the Book

Also by Max Yoho:

The Revival

Tales from Comanche County

Felicia, These Fish Are Delicious

The Moon Butter Route

With the Wisdom of Owls

Never let reality limit your life.

With the Wisdom of Owls

Max Yoho

Dancing Goat Press
Topeka, Kansas

With the Wisdom of Owls

Copyright © 2010 by Max Yoho

Reproduction in any manner, in whole or in part,
in English or in other languages, or otherwise
without written permission of the publisher is prohibited.

This is a work of fiction.
All characters and events portrayed in this book are fictional,
and any resemblance to real people or incidents is purely coincidental.

For Information address: Dancing Goat Press
3013 SW Quail Creek Dr., Topeka, Kansas 66614

www.dancinggoatpress.com

ISBN: 0970816057
EAN 13: 9780970816054

PRINTED IN THE UNITED STATES OF AMERICA
by CreateSpace.com

Acknowledgements

For Carol,
for her constant help and love.

With special thanks to
my editor, Morgan Chilson,
and my writer colleagues at A Table for Eight
for their enthusiasm and suggestions.

"With the wisdom of owls shall they spread their wings.
  And they shall fly."

— *Book of Provocations: .03215*

1

There was an owl. I'm sure of that.

It circled above my parents-to-be as a Gypsy warned them to be joined in matrimony before the cock crowed thrice. The Gypsy married them on the spot for fifty cents and all were pleased, except perhaps the cock, who became the wedding feast before he had a chance to crow thrice or consult his attorney.

Nine minutes later the owl circled above their 1947 Chevy on this, the honeymoon night—the night I was conceived. I know this—only because I know it. If you are being conceived it does not leave a great deal of time for bird watching.

So what I tell you must be somewhat guesswork, but I know the back seat was torn in a place or two. Butt sprung, because I was not the first to be conceived in that back seat. I do not wish to judge, but I would be more pleased had my mother noticed there was a little conceiving going on. In my heart I wish she could have paid attention to other things besides the damned owl circling above, but in my deep memory I know she was watching the owl.

I was born on a day of total eclipse of the sun. I was so busy I missed the whole heavenly event, perhaps a portent of what my life would be. As the light returned and my father clearly saw my face, he concluded my best hope for the future lay in frightening Jehovah Witnesses from the front door.

On the evening of my nativity I was exhausted. It was quite enough to be rousted from my comfortable sac—dodging, on the way out, unpleasant parts and pieces of my mother's secret mechanisms. It had helped to shut my eyes, but I could not ignore slippery, mother-type things nudging and begrudging my passage. With increasing frequency, I was seized by an octopus. It squeezed me without mercy, forcing me toward the exit. At length, in desperation, I jabbed it in the gut with my elbow and kneed it in what I could only hope was one of its eight groins. Throughout the next several months, though her doctors ridiculed the very idea, my mother suffered the pains and spasms of abdominal octopus. In the meantime, I was dumped abruptly, without dignity or ceremony, into a world not of my choosing.

My first night as an individual in my own right was sleepless and painful. I had plainly landed in a hostile environment, and the outlook was bleak. My umbilical cord had been immediately cut and tied off, severing me from all nourishment. Did they expect me to become a hunter and gatherer? Though I protested loudly at this affront, the worst was yet to come. And with, seemingly, no thought at all as to whether or not I could spare it, half of what made me a boy was lopped off. With that came my first real knowledge: circumcision is the price paid for lack of constant vigilance. I resolved to never allow myself the luxury of sleep lest I be snipped and scissored into nothingness; I was afraid to even blink.

From the start they called me "Harry," which was not my name at all. Thoroughly disgusted at being given such a moniker, and having no idea what *their* names might be, I decided to call them "Mother" and "Father," just to show them how it feels to be pushed around! Each time they called me "Harry," I shat, and at length, the mother started calling me, "Oh, Harry, Not Again!" which seemed to me to have a certain panache and assured that at least I would not be confused with all the other Harrys. On these same occasions, the father called me, "Oh, Hell, Not Again!" An unusual name, unique perhaps, but the only way I could tell my parents apart.

I know, now, that all mothers aspire after greatness for their sons:

be a millionaire, be the President of the United States, be the Pope! But the one I called Mother had read a book—it was her fondest wish for me that I drink eight bottles of water each day. Admittedly, she was thoughtful enough to pour it into a baby bottle, but still! It is an unshakeable argument against ever teaching girls to read. A baby whose mother tried to make him drink eight bottles of water a day probably invented the life-vest.

Early on my mother encouraged me to talk. She suggested words like "mama" and "dada"; ridiculous words, although I knew what she wanted them to mean. But I had already decided on Mother and Father, and as long as they insisted on calling me Harry, that's what I would darn well call them. Father, at least, drilled me in more useful words: "ubiquitous," "indigenous," "beveled-edge," "avoirdupois," "*Pater Noster*," "*pro bono*," "brassiere."

"Brassiere" is the word I took to my heart and it served me well. Alone, I practiced that word. I rolled it around on my tongue and tried my mouth in different positions until I mastered it; until I could whisper it or yell it as loud as the best. It is, I suggest, the most important word a baby can learn. In a roomful of adults, one may gurgle "mama" or "dada" until blue in the face, but one might just as well be a piece of Camembert cheese for all the good it does. Yet, yell "**brassiere**" at the top of your lungs, and by gosh you will be noticed. Not only will you be noticed, but every adult in the room will rush to your side and make all possible haste to satisfy your every want.

I observed, by the way, that women could quickly be trained to make a fast, unobtrusive check of their undergarments when I screamed this word. By natural progression, it seemed to me, the second word in my vocabulary must be "fly." From my deep memory I knew the average man checks his fly every one hundred and thirty-seven seconds, and more often if prompted. Thus, you will see, when I shouted "brassiere" and then "fly," adults would convulse into a ridiculous scrambling and self-patting—all the while attempting to look as innocent as an orphan's eyes. Adults are not entirely useless and can be amusing if properly trained.

Too kind and too honest to lie about my physical appearance, the minister stood dumbstruck and eyed me from the foot of my crib. "Well," he grudgingly admitted, "he is a child of God." He did not pretend that I was made in God's image. His faith was so great he knew God would have his butt for that.

"He drinks a lot of water," my mother encouraged.

The minister, knowing his approval was expected, nodded and told us the Bible has a great deal to say about water. My father segued smoothly into the fact that the flies and mosquitoes were far fewer in our house since my arrival. The minister raised his hand and said, "Bless thee, Harry." So, of course, on hearing him call me "Harry"—I shat.

The minister slunk—the only word for it, from my room; his faith, perhaps dampened, his calling, perhaps in question.

Father, now in a Biblical frame of mind, stayed by my crib cryptically misquoting the holy word. "There will always be horrors and rumors of horrors," he warned me. "Mothers-in-law!" he blasphemed. "Your Grandmother!" he blamed.

Without a doubt, two new words for my growing vocabulary, but I would not yet try them. Oh, no, I'm no fool. Not, at least, until I understood the anger, the quivering hopelessness in his voice.

He lowered his head and covered his face with his hands. "She will destroy our domestic tranquility! She will ruin my equanimity!"

"Your equa what?" I questioned.

"Nimity, Son, nimity."

"Does that mean she's evil," I pursued.

"Evil? Evil? She's an abomination!"

My thirst for understanding the curiosities and anomalies of the human species was unquenchable.

"Is one sprinkled, or immersed, when one becomes an abomination?"

"Abominations should be drowned!" he cried.

Wow! Drowning as a holy sacrament! No one understood theology like my father. But I knew I must watch out for that Mother-in-law-grandmother.

2

I have brought you along gently, only hinting at my misfortune.

I have the face of an owl! There, it's done.

Don't look away. I'm not a monster. I do have very large eyes, and my nose does somewhat resemble a beak, but I have no feathers.

Oh, yes, and you may call me "Harry."

I've stopped fighting it, stopped my useless rebellion. It was a failure. I admit it. Also it was putting too much strain on my mother. She was showing signs of martyrdom. No longer, when she changed and washed me, did she just say "Oh, Harry, not again!" She had added another bead to be used in the rosary of her incantational ritual of diaper changing. I can tell you the words, but I cannot properly describe her tone… "Oh, don't worry about me, I'll be all right."

Imagine a Christian martyr slowly roasting over a toasty fire, shouting: "Oh, don't worry about me, I'll be all right." On the outside, putting on a happy face for the crowd, but on the inside, pissed as hell. That was my mother.

With my becoming more socially, if not physically, acceptable, visitors started to arrive. One of the first was a lady introduced to me as the woman who delivered me.

It was the first time I caught my mother in a deliberate lie. I was *not* delivered! I was *evicted* like a penniless widow, tossed out, bereft of the only home I had ever known, without a stitch on my back! With only a caul over my face, which did not keep me warm. It was a sticky thing, with a smell that would gag a bedbug.

Don't try *that* on *me*, I thought. My innate wisdom told me this lady had nothing to do with my being here. Do I look like a fool? Well, yes, an owl maybe, but not a fool. I arrived in this world because of an octopus. Don't bother to tell me to forgive and forget either; I never shall. I owe that octopus and I owe it good. "This womb ain't big enough for the both of us, partner! You'd best be out of here before sundown!" Now, see, an octopus has either eight arms, and thus eight armpits, or eight legs, and thus eight groins. You do the math, as the fellow says. I was plainly outnumbered, although, I prefer to believe, not out-classed. Either way, I was gone.

Having satisfied myself this visitor was not a *deliverer*, how should I categorize her? What was her species? I fell back to the words my father was teaching me. A mere glance told me she was neither a "beveled-edge" nor a "*bon mot*," neither a "mama" nor "dada" nor a "Harry." With the swiftness of an owl, I pegged her. She was an "avoirdupois"! Sixteen "drams," sixteen "ounces"—whatever—she was certainly at least sixteen of *something*. I could also tell that at least two parts of her "something's" were probably French. A beauty spot on her cheek had failed in the only thing ever asked of it, and her dark eyebrow stretched without interruption above her nose. Maybe she was Greek. In truth, she might have been Presbyterian for all I knew, but I shuddered at the thought of her handling my innocent naked body.

At length, good manners triumphed. I grinned, favored her with my owl-eyes at their widest and shouted "**Brassiere!**"

Our guest shot my mother a quick, bewildered, questioning look. "Might he be hungry?"

"No," my mother explained, "it's just that he sometimes has trouble expressing himself. He's real good about drinking water," she added lamely.

Another lie, but this time an innocent one. I believe I expressed myself quite adequately, given the few words from which I had to choose. Mother, leaving no room for doubt, explained to my father that he was forbidden to teach me any more words. "Brassiere," she said, "is not a word that belongs in a baby's mouth."

Well, the truth of it is, it's a wonder I ever learned to talk at all. In my opinion, neither "ubiquitous" nor "indigenous" were right for my mouth. They felt like crushed gravel and tasted as if they had been poured from a funeral urn. "Brassiere," on the other hand— well, I loved the zzzzz sound. "*Pater Noster*" had possibilities, but I would likely only use it on holidays.

"'**Brassiere?**'" my mother cried. "Lord help me!"

But it wasn't the Lord who came to help her. It was Wyatt. He came to me that same night, the night of my one-month birthday. Having survived child mutilation of the cruelest kind, I was now able to sleep, and I was ready to sleep.

"Wyatt" was his name—an owl by trade. The very owl, in fact, who in my mind started this whole mess. Wyatt was not an elegant owl as one might find pictured with a pussycat and a pea-green boat in a children's poem. Somewhat seedy and shifty looking he was, and if browsing through a barrel of owls, you would find him near the bottom. But Lord, he introduced himself as my **godfather**! I guess it made as much sense as anything else did in this place. His breath was redolent of rodents and small bunnies, and a toothpick slanted from the corner of his beak.

"Don't say 'brassiere,'" he told me abruptly. It seemed an incredibly poor way to begin a conversation. I was not in a good mood anyway, and had no desire at all to spend the night with an owl that lacked the civility to even say "howdy."

"It's one of the few Human words I can say. It has served me well and I shall say it as often as I like! Brassiere, brassiere, brassiere!"

He giggled! The damned owl giggled!

In the first place, I didn't ask to be born. I didn't want to be born. Didn't I fight a stupid octopus to prevent that very thing? In the second place, I would never have chosen to be born into a world where I would have a silly, giggling owl as a mentor.

He read my thoughts, "Don't call your twin sister a stupid

octopus." he grumped. "Her name is Violet. And octopuses are not stupid, they're just very territorial.

"Now look, Harry, I'm really sorry Violet turned out to be an octopus. But it's not my fault. Sometimes things just go wrong."

"I don't like the name '*Harry*!'"

"I know. Sorry about that too. Please don't soil yourself."

"I'm trying to quit," I told him. "Anyway, what am I supposed to do now that I'm here? It's not easy living with a father who sneaks in at night and tries to make me say "bivalve" and a mother who has an impacted octopus in her belly."

But Wyatt had started to fly. "I'll be back and tell you more," he shouted.

Unable to sleep now, I pondered my new godfather. Wisdom-wise, I concluded, not all owls graduate at the head of their classes.

Daylight came again, as I had learned to expect, and with it I found two new words had been added to my repertoire. My mother used them when she discovered I had kicked my bad habit: "Well, hallelujah!"

I seemed to have a natural flair for language, and was nearly overcome with excitement when I found that by simply adding an indefinite article I could form a complete sentence. I tried it first on my mother when she arrived for my early nursing.

"Well, hallelujah! A brazzzeer!" The glissando-like intonation of the word was, of course, just showing off, but the look on her face allowed me to forgive myself. My father was plainly delighted with my new phrase and went through the house trying it himself.

I was obviously precocious, learning to talk at such an early age, and yet, my precocity seemed to cast a palpable hesitancy over my parent's pride.

It was full daylight, and I was wide-awake when Wyatt again coasted silently through my open window. Grinning like he had three peckers and would be pleased to prove it, he perched on the foot of my crib. "I have a gift for you!" he announced.

"Well hallelujah, a brassiere!" I shouted.

"Nope," he said, too full of himself to notice my new words. "It's a baby bunny." In cupped talons he held that dead rabbit as if it were a rare jewel, and offered it proudly. "Eat the head first; it's the best part."

With a grace that belied my tender age, I reminded him I had no teeth and was not yet on solid food. "Perhaps another time."

He accepted my reasoning rather too quickly I thought, and in a trice—at most a trice-and-a-half—the bunny disappeared down Wyatt's throat and the ever-present toothpick again dangled from the corner of his beak.

Unobtrusively, Wyatt sought to suck a remaining bit of bunny fur from his beak and adopt a serious mien. The unobtrusive part failed completely, and the serious mien attempt would have been received cruelly by a more discerning audience. He absolved himself smoothly for his social gaffe, spat, raised his eyebrows even farther and spoke in a somber voice: "Today we need to speak about your future. Your Mission in Life."

"You needn't bother," I told him. "My future is already planned and my Mission is set in stone. I shall climb back up there and kick my so-called "sister's" octopuscular butt out of the nest! I shall reclaim The Old Home Place. I'll call in a plumber to reattach the umbilical cord to my bellybutton. Violet is toast!"

Wyatt shook his head thoughtfully. "Maybe you'd better talk that over with your mother first."

"It won't work," I replied. "Every time I say, 'Well, hallelujah, a brassiere,' she brings me a bottle of water and changes my intimate apparel."

"Your what?"

"My diaper, Wyatt. My diaper."

"Oh, yes, well…I'm afraid you are really not communicating well at all."

"You're saying I can't communicate? For heaven's sake, Wyatt! I speak High Owl fluently, plus three owl dialects. Thanks, no doubt, to you."

He quickly denied any responsibility for my owlosity, but I noticed he had his talons crossed.

"Well, maybe something went wrong. I'm sure you didn't learn the word 'intimate' from me."

"With all due respect, sir, it seems to me that a lot of things have gone wrong under your administration."

"Look, Harry, I'm doing the best I can, ok? This is a part-time job, ok? I only signed up for this godfather-mentor thing because Owling has fallen off something terrible. There's just not much demand for owls these days. When I think back I realize I didn't plan well for *my* future. All those days I wasted trying to learn all that crap about when to say 'Who, Who, Who' and when to say 'Whom, Whom, Whom.'

"When I was an owlet I never had monkey bars to play on, I never had a sled. I want things to be better for you."

"Please, Wyatt, just stop. Nobody likes a whining owl."

"Sorry," he said. "I need to go get some sleep anyway. But first I want to give you some advice." He searched the feathers beneath each wing. "Um...I seem to have forgotten my notes. Never mind, a wise old owl always has some advice to offer. Mark it well, young Harry, there may be a quiz:

#1. When approaching another vehicle at night, always dim your headlights.
#2. Never run with a Popsicle stick in your mouth.
#3. Neither a borrower nor a lender be."

"That's it? That's the foundation on which I'm supposed to build my whole life?"

"Certainly not," he huffed. "But it's enough for today." He spread his wings and flew away.

Holy cow.

3

Despite my braggadocio to Wyatt concerning my plan to regain The Old Home Place from Violet, I realized the fulfillment of my ambition lay far in the distance. Far, too far. While I lay around waiting to grow in wisdom and stature, Violet would be making herself quite comfortable planting dahlias, maybe even erecting a picket fence. I could have wept for my mother. She would have not only an octopus in her belly but, Lord, Lord, she would not like having a picket fence in there too.

Most likely Violet was already using my warm corner of the womb as a potting shed. That bitch! Maybe she was planning a goddamn rose trellis in the uterus, or a sports complex for intrauterine games. For my mother's sake as well as my own, Violet had to go.

But both wisdom and stature seemed to come very slowly. I was strong enough to hold up my head and roll over, neither of which would exactly chill the blood of an octopus.

I had learned only a few new words of Human Speak, and I was mistaken in thinking my parents' names were "Father" and "Mother." They called each other "Darling" and "Sweetheart," seemingly indiscriminately. Except for the time Father taught me to say "brassiere." After that he became "You Dung Beetle."

As before, I practiced my new words while alone, and I practiced them diligently. I formed them into sentences such as: "Well hallelujah, Sweetheart, a brassiere!" Most of my newly spoken words brought me unabashed adoration, but with the word "brassiere" I fell abruptly from grace. Both adult humans and the Human language are difficult to understand; I could not seem to get a grasp on either.

My mother called my goo-goos, gurgles, and wazwumps "baby talk." My father assured visitors that I was speaking Cherokee. Whether he was a "Darling" or a "Dung Beetle," he was astute, and I could not but respect him. Still, astute or not, I suspected even he could not understand Cherokee. Nor could anyone else, myself included.

Wyatt was really the only one with whom I could hold a meaningful conversation. We always spoke High Owl, and so Wyatt, poor Wyatt, bore the brunt of my frustrations and complaints. He was always sympathetic but sometimes missed the point. I explained, for instance, how once, in baby talk, or Cherokee, I asked to have my diaper changed. Not understanding, my mother brought me a puzzled look, a bottle of buttermilk and a small, brass fire extinguisher.

"I can understand the puzzled look," Wyatt said, "but what in the world did you plan to do with the buttermilk and fire extinguisher?"

Though he tried to be understanding, Wyatt had little patience with such nonsense, and preferred to harp incessantly on my future. During the night he thought of three possibilities that he could approve. Cautiously, he suggested I might become a school janitor. Somehow I had the feeling he didn't like this idea any more than I. He admitted it would necessitate expunging some of the inappropriate words from my vocabulary. The children might be hard to stand, but shiny floors and the smell of all the polish were often a favorite part of his dreams.

"Or," he suggested shyly, "you could learn to make Heath Bars!" He rushed on hardly taking a breath. "See, we could live together in the woods and by night I would go 'Who? Who?' at anything that wriggled or thought about wriggling and by day (gasp) you could make Heath Bars."

Wyatt loved Heath Bars.

"But here's the kicker." He flicked an imaginary fleck of lint from his shoulder and opened his eyes to their fullest. "Here, Sir, is the absolute, goddamn kicker! The granddaddy of all kickers, the Wimbledon winner of wisdom kicking, the…"

"For crying out loud, Wyatt, stop flicking flecks and kicking kicks and tell me! I'll be on Social Security before I *have* a career!"

He straightened his body to about two inches above hubris. "You shall be a chimney sweep!"

"Did you say '**chimney sweep**'?"

"Do you have wax in your ears, son? Chimney sweep."

"Well, why under the light of the living sun would I want to be a chimney sweep?"

"You're made for the job," he said. "You can fly into any chimney, flap your feathery wings a few times, and *voilà*, the chimney is clean."

"Wyatt, I don't have feathery wings. I don't have wings at all, and I can't fly. I am not an owl."

"You will be, Harry, you will be. You look like an owl, you talk like an owl and you will be an owl."

"Good Lord," I cried, inadvertently slipping into a rarely used Owl dialect, "are you telling me I'll grow feathers? …Even in my pubic area?"

Well, I sincerely hope you never have to witness a grinning and giggling owl.

"Those pubic feathers will tickle you to death, Harry. Just tickle you to death."

Naptime brought me no respite from Wyatt's dire predictions. Sleep came with the threatening sword of eternal owldom and a feathery crotch hanging over my head. Visions of dark, terrifying chimneys and an early death caused by Black Lung Disease haunted my dreams. My own mother, repelled by my soot-covered body, was refusing to give me the warm, sudsy baths I loved, and insisted I shower in the basement. The *basement!* The very word brought images of hunch-backed ghosts and scabrous spiders, crouched and waiting to devour or deflower my tender young body. She warned me I must take my time and do a good job in the shower. If she found one tiny smidgen of soot on her clean white sheets, she would be completely pissed.

And thus it would be, day after day or night after night until, at last, my retirement. At best, I might receive a gold watch and a cardboard box of chocolate-covered mice, perhaps a pat on the back, and the words, "Well done, good and faithful owl."

One more poor wreck of a chimney-sweeping owl put out to pasture.

I woke in a sweat, with a white feather not two inches from my nose. Be damned to ghosts and spiders! I was molting!

"Brassiere!" I screamed, "Brassiere, *brassiere*, **brassiere!**"

Taking time only to grab a bottle of water, Mother rushed to my side. The God-given cure for anything from snakebite to a wheezing death of the rickets, water was the panacea. But even eight bottles of water would not stop the molting.

Obviously my mother had never molted. The sight of me screaming at the sight of a feather tickled her to death. She picked me up and tortured me with that white feather.

"Ticky, ticky, ticky," she cooed. Thanks to my hard work and perseverance, I will modestly admit to having become somewhat of an expert at spitting up, and on this day it stood me in good stead. Right down the front of her dress it went, like an owl regurgitating bones and toenails. Then, when I could catch my breath, I screamed, "Dung Beetle!"

I suppose it never occurred to her that I was only calling my father. I intended no offense, no disrespect. Nevertheless, she laid me roughly back in my crib and poured the bottle of water on my head. I found it a rather refreshing change from the way she usually administered my water. A long lecture concerning the respect one should show one's mother and the proper use of the Human language followed. The lecture was not wasted on me. I listened carefully and took it to heart.

I also picked up several new words on which I would practice at my leisure. And these, unlike the words my father liked to teach me, were good, short for the most part, and easy. Many had only four letters and pleasing sounds, some harsh and metallic, some squishy. A mother's eagerness to teach is surely a God-given and wonderful gift.

It was two days later when Wyatt again appeared, jaunty, with a new Lombardy poplar toothpick in his beak. I was still upset from my experience with the feather and in a bad mood from lack of sleep.

"Where in the world have you been?" I asked grumpily. "I've been looking all over for you."

He grinned at me, as only an owl can grin, winked at me, as only an owl can wink, and swaggered his new Lombardy poplar toothpick cockily, as only a Lombardy poplar toothpick can be swaggered.

"I've been off saving the world," he smugged.

"Bull!" I told him.

"Well," he sighed, "would you believe I saved three counties in southern Nebraska?"

There is nothing, I think, more depressing, sadder, than the sigh of an owl. But, as with many others of my generation I suppose, I wouldn't really care if southern Nebraska, all or part of it, were to be boxed-up and shipped to Byelorussia.

I explained to Wyatt all about my horrible dreams and my being ticky, ticky tickyed nearly to the point of extinction. He seemed not to hear me.

"I'll bet they are very happy indeed up there now," he mused.

"Who's happy? Certainly not me!"

"Why, those folks in Nebraska."

"Well, if the ding-bing folks in southern Nebraska are so happy, they most likely have never been subjected to a ticky, ticky, ticky by a ding-bing feather," I shouted.

"Nor have I," he grinned, "Nor shall I ever be. There's a three dollar fine for tickling an owl."

4

If you are thinking that my twin sister, Violet the octopus, had gone from my mind, you are quite mistaken. That small gland—the revenge gland—that lurks behind the pancreas in all of us, burned brightly. Its white-hot incandescence would be blinding to the eye, and the putrid, fetid odor of burning octopus flesh floated in layers throughout my abdomen. It lazed around my liver. Its sulfurous scent surged and swirled, surrounding my spleen. Its bilious breath bent and billowed behind and beyond my bowels.

Oh, no, I had not forgotten Violet.

Memories of The Old Home Place pierced my heart. I longed for those halcyon days when I snuggled in the womb dreaming of butterflies and ladybugs. Oh, that sweet place. A place with no feathers and never a bottle of water poured over my head.

From my deep memory came a feeling of discomfort, a tenacious tentacle tickling my tiny toes. Yes, there could be no doubt, it was Violet, using her octopusery to instill within me a detestation of being tickled.

Oh, no, I had not forgotten Violet.

But in a lighter vein, and on another day, Wyatt appeared bringing his two brothers: Shy Clayton and Metcalf. Fine looking owls both, richly feathered and meticulously preened. As was the case with Wyatt, both presented sparkling, golden eyes seemingly as large as the headlights of a 1933 Cadillac. If dressed in white spats and a feathery ascot, Shy Clayton might have been welcomed into the finest drawing rooms.

Metcalf looked to be a successful political boss—the man to see if you wanted a sidewalk repaired or wanted to run for alderman.

In an impressive, if unusual display of perfect manners, Wyatt removed the Lombardy poplar toothpick from his beak as he made the introductions. I, not at all expecting visitors, lay there in my soggy diaper and with some spit-up on my shirt-front. Minus his usual hyperbole, Wyatt introduced me simply as "Harry." He made no claim that I should be addressed as "*Sir* Harry" or "*Lord* Harry," and, still better, not as "*Soggy Butt* Harry."

Our conversation skirted the rocky shoals of religion and politics; we spoke of common pleasantries. The two brothers described the fine time they were having. Wyatt was showing them all the local points of interest. They dined at the grain elevator where mice were plentiful and came with side-dishes of corn, oats, wheat—your choice, and all free. Tonight they planned to eat at the Union Pacific depot where the mice had grown fat and careless. Shy Clayton announced, in an upper class though not snobbish voice, that he would only go there at night, "It simply would not do to be seen loitering around a depot."

At my first sight of them I had realized I was a lucky boy. Three wise old owls whose combined brain power could be of inestimable value in recapturing The Old Home Place. Skillfully, I maneuvered the conversation, "Seen any octopuses lately?"

Wyatt managed an embarrassed grin. Shy Clayton and Metcalf closed their owl eyes as if to become invisible. Then Wyatt saved the day and I could have kissed him.

He explained about The Old Home Place and about Violet, my twin sister the bitch octopus.

Metcalf nodded (wisely, of course) and said he had known an owl like that in Boise. "A beautiful girl," he said, "but she seemed to have as many arms as an octopus. She loved to Indian wrestle. Gypsy girl," he mused. "She'd had a beak replacement that clacked and rattled every time we kissed. She used it as castanets when she danced. Fortunately, I soon found a job in Sandusky and…"

Again Wyatt was there for me. He broke in and said that it might, indeed, be easier for me just to move to Sandusky, but I had my heart set on The Old Home Place. He said it would also be a lot easier on him to get this goal of mine settled once and for all.

"Let's make a list," Wyatt advised. "We'll need flashlights with new batteries, lots of handcuffs, one chain hoist, a cantilever, a can opener, a compass, a flame thrower, a cantaloupe…"

"Wait!" Shy Clayton said, "We'll need lariats, at least three of them."

"Good thought," Wyatt admitted. "I'll write it down."

"There's not much in the way of eats to be found there," I volunteered. "It's all piped in through an umbilical cord. We'll need to be connected."

"Right," Wyatt mumbled. "One plumber."

Metcalf had held it in as long as he could. "Flame thrower? Judas Priest! Have you ever smelled burning octopus? Look, you're going at this all wrong. For example, I guess I've captured about as many octopuses in my day as anyone here, and only once did I need a cantaloupe."

Wyatt scratched out cantaloupe. "How about wild onions then?"

"Nope," I told them, "My mother hates wild onions. They give her the hives."

"Harry," Shy Clayton said quietly, "your mother has nothing to do with this."

"You'll just darn well see how much my mother has to do with it when she starts pounding her stomach and screaming, "Get those wild onions out of there, you dung beetles!"

"Harry's right," Wyatt said. "She'll wake up the whole neighborhood." He scratched out wild onions.

My diaper had by this time dried out, so I wet it again. I believe Wyatt was the only one who noticed. Metcalf belched, and the two brothers were so close it was Shy Clayton who excused himself.

"How about cherries?"

"No way! Those cherry pits could be dangerous. First thing you know some idiot will start throwing them and then someone will get an eye put out."

"We are all too tired to think," Wyatt announced. "I suggest we each give some serious thought to this and talk again another time."

Our small council of war was an eye-opening and humbling experience for me. In my youthful exuberance and ignorance, I had never once considered how complex the dislodgment of an octopus could be. I suppose I assumed that a couple of strong, tough guys would just reach in, grab a tentacle each, and yank her out. It pains me to admit it, but never in a million years would the necessity of chain hoists and wild onions have crossed my mind. But thank God for the wisdom of owls. My mother's allergic reaction to wild onions by itself could have bollixed the whole operation.

I must be patient, I thought. I must gain wisdom. Perhaps my mother was right, and I needed to drink eight bottles of water each day. She always told me that healthy kidneys are the key to success and, try as I might, I could not name three successful gen- erals who had had weak kidneys. Well, Napoleon did have terrible hemorrhoids, but he was French.

Truth to tell, I was tired and rather glad to see the owls go. But I had made two new friends, and now had three good, wise owls for my basic cadre: Wyatt, who was solid as a rock; Shy Clayton, who could finesse us through any awkward situation; and Metcalf, who had both brains and brawn.

On this rock I would build my army.

My days passed slowly, and the brilliant glow of the absolutely unbelievable good fortune of having a son and heir named Harry seemed to be lessening in my parent's eyes. My mother sometimes brought me only seven bottles of water a day, and my father stopped haunting bookstores searching for a Cherokee to English diction- ary. He had, indeed, found such a book. It was called *The Stupid Paleface's Guide to the Noble Cherokee Language*. The author was Lump Bear. He had quit his job as a fry cook and moved to a three- story walk-up in Chicago to begin an academic life.

The sad fact is, of course, I was speaking neither Cherokee nor Baby Talk. My language of choice had become the Alsatian Striped Owl dialect. Its silver-bell-like consonants and guttural, double um-lauted diphthongs delighted me. Footnotes in Striped Owl, however, are a total bitch, so I rarely used them.

I suppose it was natural that my parent's lives would return to a more normal, perhaps dull, routine after my birth. However, I am not at all sure that I, the baby, should have been the one having post-partum depression. And was it in any way natural that *I* be the one coping with empty nest syndrome?

My mother worried constantly about putting on weight. "Do you think I'm getting fat, Harry? Now mirror, do I seem a little plump to you?" Or to my father she might say, "Lover, am I developing a bit of a tummy?"

And Lover would respond, "Lover, you are developing a *lot* of a tummy."

"Well, thank you very much, Mr. Dung Beetle! By the way, your fly is open."

"It's not my fault. I think the damn thing is broken."

"It's not broken. You just don't work it properly."

"Well, come on over here, Baby, and show me how to *work my fly!*"

"Not on your life, Dung Beetle. The last time I worked your fly we ended up with that wet diaper machine in the crib."

So the grass grew, I suppose. The postman and the milkman came and went. The postman was always as bright and cheerful as an Easter morning. The milkman was as dour as three quarts of butter-milk and a pint of sour cream. The clock was wound, sometimes six times a day, sometimes not at all. It depended, I assumed, on some astrological cycle that I was still to young to understand.

From my window I watched the clouds, often-pleasant cumulus camels or crocodiles, sometimes those as black as Evil itself, as threatening and terrifying as a carbuncle on an Archbishop's nose.

My most pleasant times were those when Wyatt came to visit. We talked, seemingly for hours and always in High Owl. Wyatt was not a linguist. Oh, he had picked up a few words of Crow Talk, but he considered that a "gutter language" and would not use those words around me.

"You'll learn enough of that when you start smoking cigars and hanging around in pool halls," he'd say.

I must tell you that Wyatt took his responsibility as a mentor seriously. He taught me many things. I will admit to being almost a total washout at algebra, learning only enough to make Violet look like a fool, if I ever had the chance. But he taught me several different ways to play solitaire, with which I could pass the time when I returned to The Old Home Place. And he insisted that I learn at least the rules of five card draw and seven card stud, in case I might want to have a few of the boys in for an evening.

As subtly as possible I tried to explain that in my little nest of a womb there was not even room to *shuffle* cards.

"Well, dammit," he growled, "after you've been there a while you might decide to build on. Yes, I love that thought! Just imagine it," he chortled, "you could have a bed womb, a dining womb, a living womb, a…"

"Just put a sock in it," I told him. "And turn your head. I wish to soil myself now."

5

My new world continued to amaze me. It confused me, bewildered me and, sometimes, left me feeling plain pissed.

Language, for example: baby children seemed to speak Cherokee or Baby Talk, or in my case Alsatian Striped Owl. Owls speak either High Owl or one of the many dialects. Zebras undoubtedly speak Zebraic, and Kangaroos, Kangaroosie. Octopuses, it stands to reason, speak Octopus, *Low* Octopus, to be sure. But perhaps we should not expect too much from octopuses. They, like Napoleon, may simply be French.

The giraffe is a pleasant anomaly. It speaks not a word. You will never hear a giraffe say, "Bless your soul," or "Damn your eyes." Jab it with a sharp stick and it will never say "Ouch!" A hard kick in the scrotum will only bring a smile. With a giraffe there is never a whimper or whine. The giraffe, I suggest, is the smartest of us all.

We must also consider "Words of Choice." It seems to me we all have favorite words, words that dot and speckle our conversations like flies on a wedding cake.

My mother's favorite word is "dung beetle." (Yes, two words, but live with it.) It is used in either the upper case as in "Dung Beetle," or in the lower case, "dung beetle." Dung Beetle is often preceded by the adjective "stupid" if a more emphatic stress is desired.

I believe Dung Beetle is my father's given name, but it is

also used to describe contrary teapots, crooked pictures or dying geraniums.

My father apparently has no single favorite word, but rather has a secret trove of words for use in anger or frustration.

To demonstrate how my parent's words worked together: suppose my father might grumble a few of his favorite words in my hearing. Then, my mother would quickly say, "Quiet, you Dung Beetle. Little pitchers have big ears."

Well, I can assure you that this particular "little pitcher" had been around the block a few times and was already quite fluent in Dung Beetle speak.

So of course, I did use Father's words, albeit in the Alsatian Striped Owl dialect, and when Mother would hear me she would say "Oh look, Father, how cute. He's trying to sing the Star Spangled Banner."

"Humph." Father would reply, "He can't carry a tune in a sealed Tupperware container."

Yes, "brassiere," my first word, was useful for many occasions. It seemed, however, to carry some taint, some mysterious shadowy "something" that could bring either smiles or frowns. When my mother told my father she was trying to wean me away from that word, he doubled over in laughter. Do you see what I'm trying to say about the strangeness of language? Why don't we just all speak the same language and understand one another? If I go through this life again, I hope to come back as a giraffe!

With Wyatt it was more a case of word detestation. As with all owls, he hated the "Who whoo ta whoo" that had been foisted on them long ago by some well-meaning human ornithologist—and that without a vote! It is an embarrassment and an abomination to any owl!

Wyatt did have his favorite words. As an owlet, he aspired to be an elevator operator, and spent many happy hours practicing "Going Up! Going Down!" It was the bane of his life that there were so few opportunities in owling to use them. He once confided to me that sometimes on the very darkest of nights, while sitting in his lonely sycamore tree, he would shout, "Who whoo's, going up?" or "Who whoo's, going down?"

To tell you the truth, I lived in a state of constant worry that he would be caught and lose his Owl license. Had Audubon heard that, he would have soiled himself.

Week after week Wyatt continued to harp about my future. "Gainful employment!"

He grumbled, hinted, shouted, preached. "You must plan ahead for *gainful employment,* else you shall spend your last days at the County Poor Farm. You will become a ne'er-do-well!" And somehow, when Wyatt said ne'er-do-well, he made it sound as if I were destined to prefer young boys.

Lord, I knew the drill well enough. I seemed to spend half my waking hours staring at the ceiling, inventing a new "life plan" just to shut him up— a "life-plan-pitchfork" to hold him at bay.

"Oh, Wyatt! Wyatt!" I might say, "I must tell you my life plan. We're talking gainful employment, Wyatt. I shall become a church bell ringer. The hours would be perfect for me. I'll work maybe fifteen minutes each Sunday morning and then go back to sleep. I can roost right there in the steeple."

Slightly dishonest? Yes. But I had learned to accommodate Wyatt's dream that I should become an owl. Warm and secure in my own heart, was the knowledge that one way or another, I would someday return to The Old Home Place.

When Wyatt preached his "Living by the sweat of the brow" sermon, I could only close my ears. Sweat of any kind was repugnant to me, but the thought of a sweaty owl would give me nightmares. When I closed my eyes and pictured myself (an owl) at the end of a church bell rope going up and down, up and down, sweat dripping from every feathery pore…well, the gorge rose in my sweetly dimpled throat.

Why me, O Lord, why me? Was anyone else being constantly pounded by gainful employment and sweat? Not my octopus sister, Violet the bitch, I'll wager. You wouldn't catch her swinging from any sweaty bell rope. She'd be lying around sated and satisfied. No worries about food or drink. No worries about a too-tight diaper... Oh, my God, can you imagine trying to pin a diaper on an octopus?

She'd be oozing fat; oozing octopus fat on my clean sheets. Her stupid umbilical cord distended from too much food. Just too, too much. Violet sweating? My soggy *butt*, she was!

So what about my father? Was he gainfully employed? You'd find no sweat on *his* brow, I'll be bound. If he labored at all, the effort was surely softened by the pleasure he derived from being my father.

And my mother, blessed with the most precious life's work of all—caring for me. It is difficult for me not to equate her with the Holy Mother, except that in my deep memory I remember the back-seat of that 1947 Chevy. I will never claim that my coming was announced to her by an angel of the Lord, but if I remember rightly, there was an owl trying to give her a strong hint.

As for the sweat on my mother's brow, it was indeed sometimes there, although I doubt if she lived by it. It occurred mostly when I shouted "brassiere" or soiled myself.

Failure to include my Godfather and mentor in these contemplations would be to fail, indeed. Wyatt's life was a success; an inevitable success to be sure, a preordained success. I cast no aspersions at all on his personal talent and ability, but predestination is predestination and an owl—after all, will be an owl.

A rose is a rose is a goddamned rose, and I'm tickled to death he had everything handed to him on a silver platter, but he didn't have to sleep with an octopus either, did he?

Doggone it, I've soiled myself again. Never mind. Sometimes I let myself get too excited.

As I started to say, I knew there were other people in the world, although I could not imagine why—I hadn't needed them at all. Their life goals must be woefully unfulfilled because upon arrival I had been supplied with a Sweetheart and a Dung Beetle to see to my wellbeing and grant my every whim.

I could only hope that someday they might all find gainful employment. Otherwise, some sweet day, an owl with a Lombardy poplar toothpick might appear with a message for them.

6

I was never sure if it was a Thursday or a Friday when I awoke to find Wyatt, Shy Clayton and Metcalf again perched at the foot of my crib. I wasn't sure because my mother had ripped the calendar from the wall that faced me. I also found, as one might say, that the harmony that usually existed between Sweetheart and Dung Beetle had turned decidedly sour.

The calendar was a gift from Al's Automotive Repair Shop. It was my father's position that the lady on the calendar would, once and for all, clear up any confusion I might have in regard to the word "brassiere."

My mother's position, stated with impeccable enunciation, was that my father was not only a Dung Beetle but also a perverted corrupter of children. Inasmuch as she wouldn't allow Al's gift calendar to remain in her house, she (kindly, in my opinion) suggested where he could put that treasure. Then, with a sort of verbal asterisk, she added a footnote suggesting that if Al had any more calendars he could ditto.

So I couldn't tell Monday from Thursday, or Friday from smoked haddock. We will, therefore, never know just when the Brothers Owl next appeared.

If you have never awakened to find six huge owl eyes staring at you not three feet from your face, consider yourself blessed. I will tell you it's probably worse than having kidney stones. I will also tell you that three grinning owls are not much better than three sweating owls.

Of course Wyatt was there with his ever-present Lombardy poplar toothpick. Shy Clayton perched pensively, only barely resigned to whatever might happen next; Metcalf smugged conspiratorially, as fat as an undertaker's dog.

With the solemnity of the rap of a gavel Wyatt shifted his toothpick, "Good, uh, morning, uh, Harry. We're here to give you your first, uh, flying, uh, 'experience.'"

"Bull!" I replied. It was as near to eloquence as I could manage. "Wyatt," I explained, trying to sound calmer than I felt, "Humans don't fly. I am a human. Neither wings nor feathers do I have—especially, as we have discussed, no feathers in my pubic area. Owls fly, magnificently, I admit. Ducks fly; pigeons fly. I do not fly."

"Harry, I consider you a chrysalis. Soon your arms will develop into wings. Your body will be covered with feathers and you will be an owl. You *will* fly!"

"And *you*, sir, are full of what gives soiled diapers a bad reputation."

"So don't thank me then already." He tried his offended, Yiddish Owl voice.

"What I'm trying to tell you is that *you* won't be the one who's flying. *We* will do the flying. You will just be the happy passenger, looking down and enjoying the world from a new perspective. Metcalf and I will each take one of your hands, Shy Clayton will take your feet and we'll carry you aloft. We'll fly around the room a few times, and you will feel like the Red Baron with a soggy diaper."

"You'll drop me on my soft spot and I will spend my life as a paraplegic, probably a Spanish paraplegic."

"Ah ha! You don't speak Spanish!" he cried in a triumphant "gottcha" voice.

"I can learn," I offered weakly.

Normally at this point, I would have screamed "Brassiere!" But thanks to Al's calendar, I knew that was not what I needed. Doubtless anticipating such a scream, Wyatt gently laid his wing over my mouth and the odor of his wingpit took the last of the fight out of me.

The attempt to lift me was like a bad storm, with the thunder and wind of wildly flapping wings and the rain of dust and feathers. Interspersed with grunts and owl-farts and someone shouting, "Try harder! You're not doing your part!" the storm raged. Still, not even a cigarette paper could have been slipped between the mattress and myself. Eternity takes forever, but at last the three of them collapsed—and I was safe.

As they recovered, Shy Clayton began chivying Metcalf about the old days when Metcalf had been a strong champion and daredevil flyer. "Do you think you could still do the old WWI Immelmann Turn?" he asked.

Metcalf chuckled. "Hell," he said, "I haven't done that for years. I likely could though."

"It would certainly be an inspiration for young Harry to see that one," Shy Clayton mused.

"By grab," Metcalf grinned, "I believe I'll give it a try! Just don't laugh if I don't get it right the first time." He stretched his wings and puffed himself out, as anyone might before doing the dangerous Immelmann Turn. Taking a few fast steps, Metcalf launched himself into the air and executed a few fancy didos. Zigging and zagging insolently, he flouted the laws of aerodynamics, bolstering his confidence and showing off.

Wyatt sighed quietly. "Awkward as a fat girl trying to pee in a Dr. Pepper bottle."

"Here goes!" Metcalf cried. He twisted, bent double, closed his eyes, gained altitude---and power-dived face first into the chiffonier.

It was one mighty dazed Metcalf who brought himself first to his owl-knees and then, finally, to his feet. He shook his fisted talons at the ceiling and cried, "May you and all of your descendents suffer the itching and embarrassment of psoriasis, Red Baron!" I knew that for today at least, the flying lessons were over.

The good-byes were hasty. Wyatt and Shy Clayton flew quietly out the window and Metcalf, crumpled beak and all, limped toward the front door, neither knowing nor caring if it was Thursday or Friday.

There was no more talk of giving me a grand tour of my bedroom ceiling. Shy Clayton and Wyatt had returned home, wherever home was. Before leaving, Metcalf protested loudly that his crash into the chiffonier was not an accident at all. He did it as an object lesson for me—so I would understand how dangerous flying could be. If that was the case, the crumpled beak and the two black eyes were most certainly acquired in vain. He was preaching to the choir.

Wyatt's concern on his next visit seemed to be my rapid growth. If I had grown so big that three strong owls couldn't lift me, he wondered, how in the world I ever expect to fit back into the womb? The thought had crossed my mind also, but I reasoned that with Violet, the bitch octopus, out and gone, there would be plenty of room for me.

"A womb," I explained, "is not like an egg. If you push on the walls a little, they will give. I'll have room.

"Tell me the truth, Wyatt, don't you sometimes miss your Old Home Place?"

"'Old Home Place,' my feathery butt!" he replied sourly. "It was a filthy prison. How would you like to be trapped in a small, unventilated Tupperware-like container half filled with green baby owl doo doo?"

"Are baby owls really *green?*" I inquired. He certainly had my attention.

His chin drooped to his breast, his head shaking slowly. "Judas H. Priest," he mumbled in disbelief, "why do I try?"

I took a small helping of umbrage, only enough to satisfy my ego, which was slightly bruised. I let it slide, knowing he *would* try again.

"I busted out of that place as soon as I was able," he continued. "Not only was it unhealthy, it was dangerous. Only an eggshell between me and sudden death. I constantly had nightmares about becoming an owlet omelet. And hot? Let me tell you I would have killed for an electric fan, even a funeral-home, hand-held palmetto fan. I tried to complain to the management, but it was no use.

"We all hatched at about the same time, myself, Shy Clayton and

Metcalf. Our mom was tickled nearly to death. She said sitting on eggs was like trying to sleep on a mattress filled with seashells."

"Excuse me," I said, "I thought the saying was 'a mattress filled with *rocks*.'"

"Rocks, seashells or pickled okra. For gosh sakes, who's going to argue with a depressed, sleep-deprived mother owl?"

"Well," I opined, "figuratively speaking, of course, I guess we all have our own octopuses to bear in life. Surely the *nest* must have been a pleasant place to be."

"It was," Wyatt replied. "It was like a second home to me. My mother was determined we three should all grow up to be wise (as all owls must be) and have at least a smattering of culture. At two weeks of age, we began music lessons using various instruments. Our instructor was an old owl named Mr. Yehudi. He was deaf as a rack of ribs, but he didn't charge because he was a sadist and loved to see parents suffer.

"For me, my mother chose the violin. It was a splendid instrument, a genuine Antonio Stradivarius, as envisioned by the Sears-Roebuck people out of Chicago, Illinois. Shy Clayton received a clarinet and Metcalf, an accordion. We were just starting to get the hang of it, as one might say, when my father declared he'd had all he could stand. He said he had no intention of raising a family of damned Screech Owls.

"He smashed my Stradivarius into two hundred and seventy-three pieces. Metcalf's accordion mysteriously suffered a collapsed lung, and Shy Clayton's clarinet was rudely thrown out of the nest without benefit of even a *pax vobiscum*. It was later found by an old Ukrainian wood gatherer and carried off as firewood to warm his family."

I was astounded and deeply hurt by Wyatt's misfortune. "Why, that's just awful," I said, scarcely able to speak.

But to his credit, Wyatt always found the bright side.

"Not really," he smiled. "I was the only owl in the forest with a toothpick, and it was a genuine Stradivarius."

In those days I was often awakened by the sound of an owl crunching a Heath Bar. Admittedly, some might find that strange, but it's really not. If you have an owl for a godfather the word "strange" is just about meaningless. Wyatt loved Heath Bars, and I'll give him this: he was always careful not to leave crumbs in my crib.

I tried to caution him about the need to brush often lest all that sugar rot his teeth, but he explained that owls have no teeth.

"It's a funny thing though," he said. "Even though we have no teeth, an unusual number of owls become dentists. That's the truth. I knew one once in New Mexico who was born with a cloven beak. He nearly starved, poor fellow. Not because he couldn't eat, you understand, but when he tried to say 'Open wide please' he just whistled through that split beak. And he always whistled the same thing: Sibelius's 'Finlandia.' His patients would finally get bored and walk out, never paying a penny. One can only stand so much 'Finlandia.'"

"Why, that's terrible," I said. "The poor fellow!"

"Yes, sir, I guess it was a gene thing. The whole family was that way: cloven beaks. I'll tell you, Harry, at family reunions it sounded like practice night at the Met.

"But wait, why so glum, Harry? You look as if you just lost your pet turtle."

"I don't have a pet turtle!" I replied with some heat. "But if I did, I would certainly do my best to lose it. I hate turtles. I hate them as individuals, I hate them in bulk, as in 'per bushel,' or 'per hogshead.' I hate them linearly, as in 'per furlong!'"

"My, my," Wyatt soothed. "Why don't you try to calm down and tell Uncle Wyatt what's bothering you?"

"I am pissed!" I said. "I am completely and irrevocally pissed."

"Um, I think the word is 'irrevocably'."

"The word is *absolutely* 'irrevocally.' I'm pissed and I'm not going to stop *talking* about it, not until this situation is irrevocably corrected."

"Well, that's better—somewhat—*perhaps*."

"It's Violet, that flower of bitch octopusery, again. What a soul-wrenching desecration of a beautiful flower and word!"

"What now?" he dreaded.

"She sent me a telepathic message. She's redecorating my womb—may her uterus roast in hell. She has spread a red-and-white checkered tablecloth over the umbilical cord and placed a Chianti bottle with a candle stuffed in it, on the top! It looks like an Italian restaurant! I suppose I should not be surprised though. Octopuses will kill for lasagna."

"Harry, Harry, You're creating a tempest in a molehill. There is surely nothing more innocuous than a checkered tablecloth. And the truth is, I, myself, am quite fond of lasagna. Anyway, I liked it better when you were grieving for your lost turtle."

"Wyatt, look me in the eye. There, good. Now repeat after me: 'There is no lost turtle; there is no lasagna.' And before you muddle this conversation irredeemably, there is also no goddamn turtle lasagna."

Unfortunately, Wyatt is one of those fellows who cannot stand to lose a debate, even when the facts are against him. He stood, smoothed his feathers, then declared he would return tomorrow when my fever had lifted and I was in a better mood.

When my mother came in to change me, she also concluded I had a fever.

"Why, Harry," she exclaimed, "I've never seen such a bad diaper rash. I always keep you so clean! I wonder what in the world caused that?"

I suppose, had I known the words in Human Speak, I might have explained that it was sometimes caused by turtles and lasagna, but I was just too tired.

7

I must not give you the impression that my only view of the world was from my crib. It was my welcome refuge, and not at all a place of confinement. I often viewed the outside world from the window of the family car car. And a fine world it seemed to be. Indeed, sometimes I felt like a veritable Amerigo Vespucci. As large as this world seemed to be, was I being terribly immodest to hope that one more continent might yet be discovered, and it would be named "Harry"? Of course, I would probably have to promise not to soil myself every time I heard the word.

And people? My soul! There were Sweethearts and Dung Beetles scurrying everywhere—a plethora of people—yet a paucity of owls.

And, in some grassy areas, there were people made of stone or bronze. These were obviously in place to be used as public toilets for birds. I took it as a sign of the good-hearted spirit of the society.

Owls, being mostly night creatures, were likely sleeping soundly and I was not surprised by their absence during the times I was out. But I was both surprised and wary at the total lack of octopuses to be seen. They being such evil, grasping things, I could only assume that everyone else had had my experience at birth, and at the first sighting of an octopus, they would fall upon it with pitchforks and cudgels. I made note of the fact that the good people of our town might be of use in ridding The Old Home Place of my nemesis, Violet.

Ostensibly, most of our outings were for groceries. "We need food," my mother would say, and off we'd go.

Our shopping trips were, for me, a wonderful learning experience; I learned things that Wyatt would never have been able to teach me.

How else, except by personal observation, would a child ever learn the true workings of a family? How else would I now know that it is the Dung Beetle's, or father's, job to sit in the front seat of the car car and turn a wheel while shouting, "Look out! You stupid son of a bitch!" Meanwhile, it was the mother's job (also sitting in the front seat, but not on the father) to shout at him, "Judas H. Priest, are you trying to kill us all?" Needless to say, I soaked up these bits of knowledge like a sponge and was eager to share them all with Wyatt.

Earlier I used the word, "ostensibly." I used it because I was not convinced we were really shopping for food. Had I just fallen off the turnip wagon? No, ma'am. Their purchases came in cardboard boxes and round, cylindrical tin cans, certainly not food as I knew it. They did not resemble, even in the most remote way, the containers in which my sustenance had arrived for the last few months.

I find I fail here. The ability to describe the two vessels, personal parts of my mother in which I found both food and drink, defies my poor efforts. Rarer than silver or the finest gold they were. And each was crowned with a jewel from which my young mouth took its delight. Their softness and texture, their unbelievable beauty, was beyond enchantment. I knew I would worship what my mother called 'din-dins,' even into my dotage. Din-dins lacked only the automatic waste disposal system to be far superior to the umbilical cord.

I viewed what my parents ate—the potatoes, carrots, and squash— in awe. If these were to someday become a part of my diet and be served to me, how in the blue-eyed hell would my mother load those din-dins? There could be no question though: I would never be able to eat a watermelon.

And so our family excursions filled me with exuberance. I was becoming a man of the world. I could truthfully claim to be one of those who had been "around the block a few times," that it was the same block time after time—well, I did not let that bother me. I had "seen the elephant!" Maybe tomorrow I would yank its tail.

8

She was there, suddenly and without warning. Very *there*, swooping me up in her arms and cooing, "Oh, Harry, you precious thing! (which I already knew). I'm your grandmother, your own mother's mother. I come from far away Austin, Texas, area code 512. You may call me 'Grandmother.'" I scarcely had the time, but I wet myself on the way up.

Adults expect a baby to be wet and seem disappointed when they are not. It's a "gotcha" moment for them and I believe it reinforces their feeling of superiority. It's a small thing but no trouble, and it keeps them happy.

"Is it all right if I give him a sip of my beer?" she yelled. "Give Grandmother a great big Texas-style smooch."

Evidently Grandmothers are for drinking beer and covering their mouths with a horrible red goo which they smear, with great delight, on helpless babies. It has the effect of inducing vomiting, and it worked.

As I have observed with all human people, Grandmothers are very deficient in language skills and speak only Human. This one's favorite words seemed to be "beer" and "Austin, Texas, area code 512." Pleasant enough sounding words, and I soon added them to my Human vocabulary. It was just a guess on my part, but, as was the case with Napoleon, she was probably French. She made, however, no mention of hemorrhoids.

Father stepped up behind her: "Looks a little like an owl, doesn't he?"

"What an awful thing to say about your own son!" Grandmother sputtered. She allowed a delicate drool of beer down onto her chin, then retrieved it with her long, Texas tongue. "He's beautiful. He's, um, well, he's one of God's children!"

"I think he looks a lot like your brother, Charles—kind of owl-faced."

"Charles does not look owl-faced, thank you very much." Grandmother took a deep swig of beer, caught her breath and belched loudly in his face. "Charles just looks like one—uh—of God's children."

Father usurped the bottle of beer, drank deeply, and replied, "It's a thing to ponder. If we are all God's children as we are led to believe, then why don't we all have owl-faces?"

Grandma shrugged, laid me back in my crib, snatched her beer back, and flounced out of the room leaving a trail of dark imprecations floating in her wake.

My crib was my place of refuge, and never more than on that day. In the next room, the discussion continued loudly. I picked out the words "owl-faced," "God," and, "your side of the family."

From the window there came a soft scratching, and when I looked, I saw four extra-large, questioning eyes staring in. The question in those eyes was: "What in the world was that?" Wyatt and Shy Clayton glided in without a sound, without even a ruffle of air.

Wyatt pointed his wing at the door and whispered "What in the world was that?"

"That was a grandmother, *my* grandmother. Her name is 'Grandmother Area Code 512.'"

"And what does one do with a Grandmother Area Code 512?" Shy Clayton asked reasonably.

I could only admit that I had no idea whatsoever. "But the really exciting news is this," I told them. "According to my father and Grandmother Area Code 512, I am a direct descendent of God."

"Phooey, and double phooey!" Wyatt exclaimed. "Just like Jessie James and his gang used to hide out in my great-great grandfather's pine tree. It's what they call an 'urban legend,' Harry. Except, I suppose, in my case it might more properly be called a 'forest legend,' and in your case a, um, maybe a 'heavenly legend.'"

"Excuse me," Shy Clayton petitioned shyly, "I believe that anything coming from heaven is called a 'revelation.' Therefore, what Harry has is likely a 'revelationary legend.'"

"Good grief," Wyatt muttered. "Whatever."

"We must be careful what we say," I cautioned. "Get Him pissed and 'Dad' might just zap us with a bolt of lightning."

Wyatt looked completely annoyed, and when annoyed, he looks like Queen Victoria wearing oversized glasses.

"Wyatt," I asked, "are you in a foul mood? Maybe even a foul fowl mood?" I was the only one who giggled. "Anyway, where is good old Metcalf?"

A long look of embarrassment passed between the brothers, and finally Wyatt spoke. "Metcalf is, shall we say, *unavailable*. He was hauled before the Grand Council of Owls and charged with taking 'inappropriate liberties' with a female owl. Fortunately, it was a fake, plastic owl placed beneath the eaves of a house to scare away barn swallows. Else he would now be rotting in the slammer.

"Hell, Shy Clayton has been dating that owl's sister for three weeks and noticed only that her paint was slightly peeling and she was very quiet for a woman. At any rate, all they could do was censure the poor boy. They threatened to revoke his Wisdom Certificate and forbade him from going courting without his glasses. Then, giving him a metaphorical slap on the wrist, they ordered him Confined to Nest for ten days, for 'dumbness.'"

"Holy H. Cow." I sighed. "Do you suppose they would trade Metcalf's freedom for a Grandmother Area Code 512?"

"Not a chance," Wyatt said. "They're an unforgiving bunch of stuffy old birds."

"Might one say that they are—'stuffed owls'?" I inquired innocently.

"Good grief to the fourth power," Wyatt growled. And away the brothers flew.

9

It is absolutely true that twins have a special relationship. This truth exists even when one twin slightly resembles a handsome owl and the other is a bitch octopus. It is a mysterious telepathic connection that renders keeping a secret impossible. Would it were not so.

I'm sure Violet (the octopusical one) enjoyed this very much. She was privy to all of my deepest thoughts and secret plans. She was, therefore, aware of my intent to invade The Old Home Place and kick her fat butt out in a most unpleasant manner. And *I* knew she was erecting sandbag-breastworks and placing fire extinguishers close at hand. Evidently, given the fire extinguishers, she had missed the war meeting where Wyatt, Shy Clayton, Metcalf and I decided against using flame throwers and wild onions in our invasion.

The fact is this: each day I was noticing a lessening of strength in the telepathic wave signal I was receiving from Violet. Perhaps it was due to the increasing distance in the time since my birth, or my continuing assimilation of human (therefore lesser) abilities.

As an instance, I might suddenly be aware of a Violet thought: *Today I shall once and for all rid myself of…*and the signal would fade away, be lost, gone, like the dying wisp of a breeze. Be rid of what? Of whom? I wanted to scream, and sometimes did. Had she dreamed up some diabolical plan for my untimely demise, or were her thoughts concerned only with smashing a cockroach?

Yet, one constant vision remained (I use the word "vision," although it is the desecration of a beautiful word): I always knew when Violet polished her nails.

Fingernails? Toenails? A debate would be endless. Or shall we, then, call them "tentacle nails"? That would likely be more acceptable to the ever-critical Octopusologists. May God save you all from such abhorrent visions, and from all bitching, nit-picking Octopusologists.

It occurs to me only now that she was putting extra effort into sending me this particular image, a straining, grunting, spiteful effort. It could be that she had raised all of her tentacles skyward, antenna-like, until her signal could have been received in Paraguay.

But no, in my telepathic mind's eye, I saw her sitting on the floor, tentacles extended in all directions, taking up every crowded inch of womb room. Hunched-over is the way I saw her, bright red paint on an applicator. Complete concentration. Oh, gently, oh, delicately, oh, the secret feminine delight of displaying her painted toenails to a breathlessly expectant, admiring world! And I could hear her, singing softly to herself, an ancient octopus toenail-painting chant, 'Gurgeldy-slurp-grunt, Gurgeldy-slurp-grunt.' Sharps and flats rubbing together like rusty steel wool.

Had she closed the window blinds? Not at all. Sad to say, but all octopuses are exhibitionists. They revel in showing the rolls of fat around their bellies, and their long skinny legs. In my deep, deep memory, I can still see her wearing fake eyelashes and a jaunty pillbox hat. But her intent was not only to offend *me*, she would be greatly pleased to also offend the intestine that occupied the space just across the abdomen. He was a peeping-tom intestine, shunned by all in the neighborhood. Unwary or uncaring, one could always see his curtain pulled slightly awry, ever watching, watching. I will admit to having had unchristian thoughts about that foul smelling organ myself, but the purposeful display of Violet painting her toenails before him? That was a mortal sin.

Oh, I knew many things were going on in Violet's mind. On a good day, when atmospheric conditions were at their best and telepathic signals were flowing freely, I could read Violet's wicked thoughts. Oh, yes. And, although not as disgustingly sickening as the painting of her toenails, more frightening by far were her delusions of grandeur. In her grandiose private world, Violet saw herself as an Empress! It's true: **Empress of the Abdomen**. With my expulsion, she gained complete control of the womb and all its luxuries. The sumptuous viands offered day and night by the bounteous umbilical cord, the silk-like cushion of love whereon one found only glorious repose and dreamed only beautiful, lavish dreams of the future:

> *This abdomen is such a jumble, and so inefficient! Only I can bring the efficiency, the order and the elegance it deserves and I demand. The liver? A little to the left, I think. The pancreas might look nice with a gilt mirror above it, and the intestines must be enclosed in highly polished copper... I can explain it as a sculpture. So much to be done!*

Now see, had I been the one who designed the human woman, I would have put a small window, an inspection plate, if you will, in the belly. That way, a woman could keep an eye on what was going on. Goodness knows, had my mother any idea at all of what Violet had planned for her abdomen, she would have had a total shit fit.

10

Lest I be misunderstood, I must tell you that Violet was not the only one on my mind. This growing "older and wiser" was, maybe, more trouble than it was worth. My head was swelling with information. Perhaps dangerously so. I learned new things every day about the people I knew: my mother and father for instance.

My mother, for example, might be explaining my father's daily absences in the typical human way, by not explaining them at all.

"Dada has gone to work work."

Good grief! All right, I could make an educated guess as to who Dada might be, but "work work"? Was he sitting in the car car practicing cursing other drivers? Was he in the basement workshop shaving his armpits, or was he following some secret desire to yodel with frogs?

It all added yet another load to my burden of learning. Did I really need to know? Still, it was all soaking into my head.

And there was, of course, Wyatt. Wyatt was the steadfast type, serious, yet with an English sense of humor, which is probably an oxymoron. He found delight in flying around my window in the dark of night crying, "Who? Who? Who has a soggy butt?"

He would do this to frustrate and annoy me until I (having no better weapon at hand) would throw a bootie at him through the open window.

This, by the way, I believe to be the origin of the now popular phrase, "Useless as throwing baby booties at an owl." If this is indeed the case, I am proud to have contributed a phrase to the Human vernacular.

Shy Clayton was a pleasant enigma. I believed him to be a Quaker but, in as much as we never discussed religion, I could not be sure. Sometimes he seemed to be leaning toward the Hindu persuasion and when I would say, "Holy cow!" Shy Clayton would admonish me, "Don't take Its name in vain."

His opinions were always well thought out, but subject to abrupt change. Sometimes he would snicker a bit at the opinions of others but then end up in total agreement. Still, Shy Clayton was a good owl to have around.

And Metcalf? Now there was an owl! He was gruff on the outside, but owl-soft on the inside. It pains me to use the past tense when speaking of Metcalf, but he was no longer the owl I first knew—always with a "traveling salesman" joke on his lips and a heart full of confidence. A sad case indeed, he suffered deep chagrin when brought down by an enemy chiffonier while attempting the tricky Immelmann Turn. Then, all too soon, his ego was crushed and his heart broken when his one True Love proved false. As Leander Kipling so aptly put it:

> Far better to be spurred in the bowel by a rowel,
> Than be shunned and scorned by a plastic owl.

Still in all, Metcalf was improving. I watched him closely, hoping for the best.

At last, for my education allows no exemptions, we must consider the many things I had to learn about Grandmother Area Code 512. Due to my great-grandmother's failure to take precautions and move to someplace like Kansas at the first sign of pregnancy, 512 was born in Texas. For that there is no immunization and no cure, no soothing draught. It is the only disease in which the sufferer takes pride in the affliction, and from all accounts, Grandmother Area Code adapted nicely.

She drank her beer from long-necked bottles.

And when there was a task to be done she treated it as one more stump to be pulled from the hard Texas soil. When Grandmother shouted, "Grab a root and growl," I'll guarantee there weren't any slackers.

Once old 512 said to me, "Son, I'm stringy as a longhorn too long on a prickly pear diet. I'm tough as a pissed on boot, and I'm here to tell you that it's time for you to stop wetting yourself!" And, by golly I did, immediately. It took three days of kidney dialysis to save my life.

My father demanded that Grandmother Area Code 512 be hauled before a magistrate and charged with *Interrupting the Flow of a Minor*, but my mother told him to just shut up before he had to be put on one of those machines himself.

Of course, there was much, much information soaking into my head and if, as I have heard, a little knowledge is a dangerous thing, what irreparable damage might *too much* knowledge cause to my head?

I presented my problem to Wyatt and asked if I would likely blow a head gasket.

"Nope," he said, "with you...," and he looked pointedly at my diaper, "...you are much more likely to blow an exhaust manifold gasket."

It was not at all due to any magnanimous proclivity for forgiveness that I forgave Wyatt his rude and vulgar comments and opinions concerning my exhaust system. Suddenly, such picayune thoughts were driven from my mind; driven away by Sweet Little Girl, a beautiful child who was suddenly placed beside me in my crib.

"Harry," a strange voice said, "this Sweet Little Girl has come to visit you."

"My soul," I thought, as I looked her over, "surely an inadequate name!" Yet still, what better words could ever be found to describe her? I searched my mind through all of the languages I knew: Human, High Owl and all of the owl dialects with which I was acquainted. No words could come close to describing her beauty.

Her head was bald as an Aspirin tablet, and she had not a tooth in her head. She was beautiful. I realized, of course, that aging is the sad though inevitable fact of life. Someday she would have both hair and teeth, but I knew I would still love her. The precious little scab on her tummy-button, I'll take my oath, just begged to be kissed. And her face! Her face might someday launch a thousand rubber duckies.

Although I wanted nothing more in life, I soon found that we could not communicate; we had no common language. Ah, God, there was so much for us to discuss, so many questions, so many feelings to share. Had she, too, been rudely evicted from her warm home by an octopus? What were her feelings concerning owls? Had she already noticed that I had the beginnings of hair on my head? Would she make unkind jokes behind my back because my mother combed my hair in such a way as to cover my bald spot? In profound frustration, I turned to her, farted, and spit-up over most of her.

And she, my Sweet Little Girl, doubtless prompted by nature and love, reciprocated exactly and immediately.

Say what you will, Love *will* find a way! It was in this manner we two forged our bonds.

At that time I would have readily wagered my soul that not even the Hounds of Hell could have separated us, but our mothers, using mystic incantations such as, "Holy shit, look at this mess!" and "Judas H. Priest,"— did.

Amid snickers of, "They say love has to be messy to be good," Sweet Little Girl and I were stripped and scrubbed. And we lay naked, side by side without a tinge of embarrassment, as happy and sweetly innocent as were Adam and Eve on their first day in the Garden.

At the first glimpse I was appalled. An abominable, even criminal act had been committed, and I was bearing witness. Her circumcision had been a disaster! While I had been allowed to retain at least a stump, my poor Sweet Little Girl was left with nothing at all. It was simply *gone!*

Even granted the greatest agility and nimbleness, she would never know the joys of writing her name in snow or adding a column of three numbers, or feel the triumph of doing yellow long division. Still, I knew that love would find a way. Perhaps I could hold her aloft and aim her. Yes! And by all that's holy, I would! I would make myself so strong that I could hold her and aim her until she could even do that most difficult feat, snow-peeing-wise, placing a decimal point at the right place and without making it look like a comma.

She would, someday, I'd be bound, write the Preamble to the Constitution. With proper punctuation!

Perhaps I was to blame, such was my conceit, but I was under the impression that Sweet Little Girl had been placed beside me as a gift. So when her mother lifted her from the crib, both Sweet Little Girl and I screamed in outrage. Not surprisingly perhaps, in my fury I reverted to my first words of Human Speak: "Brassiere!" I shrieked, "*Dung Beetle!*" But to no avail. The Indian-giver mother laughed long and loudly, but it was plain to see that her heart had hardened against me.

"Wave bye-bye, Sweet Little Girl. Wave bye-bye to Harry."

Sweet Little Girl was gone as quickly as she had appeared. With the cruelty of a Mayan priest, the mother had torn out my still-beating heart. But my heart's blood spilled not on the altar of a heathen god; my heart's blood flowed out on the pitiless altar of love.

Wyatt stopped by later in the day and found me with red, swollen eyes and a downcast mien.

"What ho, young Harry. Why do I find you with red, swollen eyes and a downcast mien?"

With a lump in my throat, I explained in as few words possible that I had found and then lost the only girl I could ever love.

"Well, dog doo," he said from his heart. "I'm truly sorry to hear that."

Summoning a stiff upper lip that almost refused to be stiff, I asked, "Wyatt, is that a new toothpick?"

"It is," he said. "It's a birthday gift from Shy Clayton, a genuine piece of the True Cross. He brought it back from Arkansas."

"That's great." I fought back my tears. "How do you like it?"

Wyatt sucked deeply on the new toothpick and replied thoughtfully, "It's sort'a sweet and sour," he said. "Sort'a sweet and sour."

My eyes drooped closed even as Wyatt still perched there, doubtless contemplating the propriety of using a toothpick made from the True Cross. In my dream I was huddled with Sweet Little Girl back in The Old Home Place. Nearby, perhaps in the shade of the ancient epiglottis, an oud was playing softly—and the womb was paradise enow.

We were connected by a cleverly contrived Y-shaped umbilical leading to our tummies. She turned and smiled at me, and at the corner of her precious mouth there sparkled a tiny jewel of spit-up.

Oh beauty, thy name is Sweet Little Girl.

11

Morning brought a rude and abrupt awakening. My first thought was that Grandmother Area Code 512 had somehow managed to get her din-din caught in the washing machine wringer. It had to be that or the sound of Armageddon. Gone was the soft oud music. Gone was Sweet Little Girl.

It was indeed old 512; she was in the living room creating a rock-solid, unassailable argument in favor of crucifixion. The desecration and defamation of Jimmy Rodgers, the singing brakeman, was happening right in our own living room. For Grandmother, his song "T's for Texas" served as doxology, national anthem, scherzo or fugue. But mostly it served as a good old soul-releasing outburst of the joy of a broken heart. Eleven-second intermissions granted brief relief as she removed her dentures for the yodel; otherwise I believe she would have eaten her face. That song fit my mood perfectly.

Wyatt always swore Grandmother Area Code 512 was a few shingles shy of being able to fix the roof. But Shy Clayton, being the gentle and patient owl he was, pointed out that she was, after all, a Texan, and therefore more to be pitied than censured. Nonetheless, even he admitted the battle of the Alamo would have had a different outcome had Grandmother Area Code been yodeling from the ramparts.

When Area Code 512 had finished her sunrise Matins and laid her thankful guitar aside to cool, Wyatt and Sly Clayton removed their talons from their ears and came in through the window.

"What ho?" Wyatt cried cheerfully. That greeting no longer bothered me. It was not a test. I had finally figured out this customary greeting was a rhetorical question. Had an answer been required, I would have been found wanting. What were my choices ho-wise? I suppose I could have shouted, "Tally ho!" but that didn't make any sense to me either. What the hell was a "tally?" And, for that matter, what the hell was a "ho?" I could have welcomed Wyatt with a Santa Claus Speak, "Ho, Ho, Ho," but, season wise—what with the window open and all—it did not seem apropos.

The echoes of Grandmother Area Code 512's yodeling hung throughout the house like motes floating on a Texas miasma. And so, with my mind clogged with yodeled motes, I just tipped my imaginary Stetson to Wyatt and said, "Howdy, partner."

I should mention at this time that, in those early days of my life, what with the difficulties of learning Human Speak, I really didn't know the difference between a Stetson and a Studebaker, nor the difference between an esophagus and a sarcophagus. But Wyatt didn't seem to notice. He was (rather ostentatiously, I thought) once more sucking on his good old Lombardy poplar toothpick. It seems that during a fit of sneezing caused by some spoor wafting by on a malevolent zephyr, the True Cross toothpick had been bitten in two.

Wyatt, being the good brother he was, had given Shy Clayton back the two pieces of the True Cross toothpick to be glued together in the form of a Christian cross. Shy Clayton had joined the two pieces and then hung it around his own neck.

It was one of those cases that defy all understanding, but Shy Clayton shortly found himself flying circles above a revival tent. And hearing a strident female evangelistic voice shouting "Who, Who, Who will come to the altar of our Lord?" Shy Clayton made the natural mistake of believing some nubile young owl was proposing matrimony to him. In a trice he swooped down to check out the action, and before he could say, "shit and goddamn," he had been Pentecostalated. Either fortunately or unfortunately, depending on how one looks at it I suppose, the necklace cum decoration, working in conjunction with, or opposition to, Shy Clayton's Adam's apple, caused the cross to behave in such a manner that many attending the revival considered it a miracle.

Wyatt explained that was the reason why he and Shy Clayton had been frantically waiting outside my nursery window. It was a terrible choice: either risk being yodeled to death by Grandmother Area Code 512 or risk being mobbed by repentant sinners who would likely pluck Shy Clayton nude to acquire his holy-relic feathers.

Finally Metcalf showed up at the window and announced it was safe for Wyatt and Shy Clayton to come out. He said the sinners repented their repentance and were going to work in a little more sinning.

It was just as well they left. Grandmother Area Code had just gargled two long-necked bottles of beer and was fine-tuning her guitar.

The day I learned to sit upright by myself looked to be a grand day indeed. Rain splattered aggressively, petulantly, teenagerly, as if thoroughly pissed at being required to work in such weather. Fat drops made a fearsome noise as they sacrificed themselves against the window hoping for a better tomorrow. Lightning promised the end of the world and thunder echoed, "Bet on it!"

Dung Beetle, in the name of all music lovers, had broken Grandmother's guitar with a strong whack across the coffee table. And Grandmother, rightly or wrongly, had taken it personally and broken Dung Beetle's collarbone with a strong whack from a long-necked beer bottle.

Mother, aka Sweetheart, judging from the sounds coming from the kitchen, was preparing lunch by running Mason jars filled with marbles through the blender.

These warm, endearing sounds of home filled me with well-being. I have never been comfortable when things got too quiet. From sheer boredom I had learned to scream and cry until Sweetheart would come rushing in and ask, "Why, Harry dear, what can the matter be?"

I wanted to say, "Please may I have a train wreck? At least a circus?" I could have explained my wants with no trouble at all had she only taken the time to learn High Owl, or at least Alsatian Striped Owl.

I will never fault her for not *trying* to be a good mother, though. If given the time, before I return to The Old Home Place, I will try to instill in her just what is important in life, and what is not.

But on this day, despite a fine beginning, the afternoon brought a preternatural quiet and I was left alone to amuse myself as best I could. Had I already exhausted all of the potential of my young life? I forced myself to face the facts, performing bodily functions is well and good, and I often derived a good deal of pleasure from it. Still, it's not something on which one can build a life.

The more I thought about it, the more the idea of unsupervised adventure began to fill me with pleasure. The possibilities, after all, must be almost boundless. I did not doubt that I had above average intelligence. Surely my language skills proved that. I admitted to myself I was going on five months old and it crossed my mind that I was not getting any younger. Still, I felt young at heart, my bones were not yet brittle and my mouth showed no signs of growing the unseemly teeth that adults so often have. It was time for me to get on with my life; time for me to make my mark in the world.

With many grunts and groans and, possibly, a slightly sprained left shoulder, I found myself in a sitting position—regarding the world from a new perspective. My back had yet to develop enough strength to hold me completely upright like a tin soldier, so I sat, hunched over, like a fat little Buddha. My head wobbled dangerously on what surely was an insufficient neck but, with my innate pluck and courage, I steadied my nerves and smiled at the world. And, my word, there, right in front of my eyes, I beheld my belly-button! That had to be it! So many times I had explored it with my fingers, rather idly. I admit I hoped I'd find screw threads or connections that would reconnect me to the umbilical cord when I returned to The Old Home Place.

I stared with bewildered incomprehension. I waited, silently pleading for at least a wink from that blind, Cyclopean eye, but none came. At length, a benevolent angel laid a wavy gossamer of tears across my eyes, attempting to shield me from what I knew to be true: there was no screw-thread, no simple push-pull connection, neither plug nor receptacle. There could be no doubt. Just as I had lost most of my boyness, some son of a bitch had circumcised my bellybutton.

With the exceptions of my birthing day and that sad, sad day when I lost my beloved Sweet Little Girl, this was the worst day of my life. And then it got even worse. I remembered seeing the sweet little scab on Sweet Little Girl's bellybutton and realized that she also had suffered multiple circumcisions. She, also, was cruelly bereft of any umbilical connection.

With the weight of my new knowledge weighing heavily upon me, I allowed myself to topple over and curl into a fetal position. I knew I would never give up my plan to spend forever with Sweet Little Girl in The Old Home Place, I just hoped to hell she liked Chinese carryout.

12

I have always believed something good was lost when folks started ignoring the common courtesy of calling to inquire if it might be an appropriate time to visit. Usually I am wet and often disheveled, often asleep. Certainly not at my best to receive guests. But the day I met Pumpkin I was clean, and dry; about as sheveled as one might ever hope to be.

Grandmother Area Code 512 stopped in my room for a brief visit, bringing me "a nice piece of peanut brittle." She often brought me whatever gift she was inspired to feel appropriate. It might be an ashtray marked, "Souvenir of Fort Worth." It might be a representation of Sam Houston carved from a peach pit or rattles from the tail of a Texas snake. The self confidence she felt in her own good taste was such that if she found an item delightful, then only a clod or a dolt would find it otherwise.

I once asked Wyatt's advice regarding the proper, courteous way to accept these gifts, and I believe his suggestion was sound:

"Take it with both hands and drop it once. She will say, 'Woopsi doodle, Y'all,' pick it up and return it to you. You must always try to make joyful noises, even if it's a piece of longhorn dung. Remember it comes from Texas and is, therefore, sacred. See now, the first thing you do is rub it in your hair. Then hit your face with it a few times to prove that you are too dumb to find your mouth. Then, when you— poor dumb Harry—appear, against all odds, to actually find your mouth, you must bite it and suck it and say, 'Ga, ga ga.' All grandmothers love and expect this. It works every time."

Wyatt sometimes took a circuitous route on the road to wisdom, but in this case, he was, as they say, "right on." Once again, his wisdom had shown as bright as a diamond in a goat's butt.

I tried this advice with the peanut brittle and it worked like a charm. Old 512 walked away with a smile on her face and doubtless a warmth in her heart, knowing she was the best gol' dang grandmother north of Lubbock and ready to spit on the boot of any galoot who doubted it.

When I finally got the sticky stuff somewhat loosened from my fingers, I tucked it away in my diaper and tried to relax my mind by thinking pleasant thoughts.

In all honesty, my mother never seemed to find as much pleasure in changing my diaper as I might have hoped. And on this day, any pleasure there might have been hit rock bottom. "Oh, my God!" she cried. "Sweet loving Jesus!" In one quick lunge she grabbed the dog-eared copy of Dr. Spock, and the pages fanned up a proper breeze as she searched for *doo doo, petrified...*

At any rate, when the doorbell rang unexpectedly, I was clean, dry and free from all traces of petrified doo doo. I was dressed in a new corduroy jumpsuit, and the Queen of Rumania would have turned green with envy had she seen ol' Harry.

And the King? The King would have rent his own garments in shame and offered me half his kingdom and his daughter's hand for my raiment. On Wyatt's advice, I would have held out and insisted on the whole daughter or no deal. But there my beautiful daydream was interrupted... and just when it was getting good.

With no introductory ceremony at all, "Pumpkin" was plopped down beside me. The "plopper," the mother of the "plopee," was a friend of my mother. A red-haired woman, her stern face announcing to the world that she would brook no unplopping of anything she saw fit to plop.

Like her mother's, Pumpkin's hair was red. But rather than lying obediently and unquestionably plopped, Pumpkin's tendrils writhed and squirmed until she might well pass as a daughter of Medusa.

At least a drum roll would have been appropriate, and an appearance by the Marine Band would not have been out of order. Pumpkin was that kind of girl.

One glance told me that here was a girl for whom an all-day sucker wouldn't last five minutes.

I can't honestly say I was glad to meet her. I believe I mentioned earlier that unexpected guests tend to irritate me. Still, I knew even then that I must behave as a gentleman. Wyatt always says, "Good manners are the gold standard of life." So I proffered the hand of friendship, which she ignored, preferring instead the death-grip of a nose grab.

I have had my nose grabbed before, but never by someone who obviously worked out in the gym with an anaconda. When Wyatt's brother, Metcalf, announced his intention of becoming my God-owlcle, he presented me with the gift of a "Junior Gang Member" switchblade knife. I now deeply regretted having refused it. Today I just might need it.

My cries of pain and astonishment soon brought succor. Pumpkin's mother rushed in and pried the painful little fingers from my nose. Nevertheless, instead of crushing her skull, as I had hoped, she merely kissed the girl and told her to, "Play nice."

Then she patted my head and said, "There, there," a useless and insulting term if ever there was one.

But Pumpkin seemed to have a primal predilection for going for the nose. She tried again, but this time I was ready. I kicked her in the belly, offering her the suggestion that nose grabbing was socially unacceptable. When she made an even more determined grab, I kicked her again, this time harder, and addressed her in the New Guinea Hairy Owl dialect. I'm sure a real New Guinea Hairy Owl would have laughed aloud at my awkward and unsure usage. But my message was simply this: "Good manners are the gold standard of life!" At least that's what I hoped I said.

I was as surprised as she was. I had never before heard of the New Guinea Hairy Owl, or indeed, of its special dialect. I could only assume that, as with my other owl languages, it came from some deep, perhaps ancient, memory.

It was a slimy, sibilant tongue, slurpy-sucky, as one might expect from gaseous bubbles rising from primordial mud. And if languages can have an odor, the gas from these bubbly nouns and verbs might have been brought from the depth of the bowels of the earth—a warning tongue, a *Don't Tread On Me* tongue.

Pumpkin gave me a rather insolent, challenging look, so I raised my foot for another kick. Then her reddish, almost translucent eyebrows lifted a bit, and the light of understanding brightened her face. Her insolence gave way to a tentative, hopeful smile. I believe that with another belly-kick or two she could have become a fine linguist.

By lunchtime we were friends. Pumpkin, being a little older than I, began with a silver spoon filled with what appeared to be a mishmash of ostrich aspic. I, determined to establish my urban sophistication, nipple-nuzzled, testing the bouquet, swirled a taste of the mother-nectar on my tongue and nodded my approval to the server. Finally, well surfeited, we properly showed our gratitude and appreciation with loud and messy burps.

Next, of course, came the changing of the diapers. As you may well have guessed, I was waiting for this moment. To my horror, I found that Pumpkin was made exactly like Sweet Little Girl, and, like Sweet Little Girl, Pumpkin would never know the pleasure of recreational peeing. There could be no doubt, no coincidence—it was not just another slipshod circumcision.

I, beyond question, set the standard for infant configuration. And therefore, I concluded, the earth had been invaded by mutants! I knew my world was forever changed. Girls were different!

When I woke the next morning the sun was barely up. Wyatt, having knocked off work a little early, was perched in his usual place at the foot of my crib.

"Wyatt," I cried, "you're not going to believe this, but girls are not at all like boys!"

He looked me straight in the eye, obviously wanting to believe me but finding it difficult. Then, pulling a long face, and sober as a quinine tablet, he said, "I'll be damned!"

Wyatt settled himself into a sitting position on the crib rail, crossed his legs in an avuncular manner, and said "Now, just exactly what else have you learned about girls, Harry?"

Looking back now, with so many months of life behind me, I realize that at that time I didn't really know much at all about girls. But at that young time, I believed, as all young men do, that I knew everything about everything.

"Girls like to eat ostrich aspic," I told him with a confidence that now embarrasses me. Wyatt gave me a wise nod, obviously relieved that this was one thing he would not need to explain.

"And," I added in a new, deeper voice that I hoped would add authority to my wisdom, "they must be kicked in the belly if one would gain their attention. I believe that if they are learning a new language, they should be belly-kicked on an 'as needed' basis and, when studying the subjunctive mood, many kicks will prove beneficial."

It would be wrong for me to deny that Wyatt was impressed.

We sat there, Wyatt and I, considering the mysteries of girlity, and that's when it came to me: a golden, sun ripened, seedless epiphany!

Pumpkin was the perfect vehicle by which I could retake The Old Home Place! There would be no need for the shackles, frogmen, flame-throwers or the gone-bad potato salad I had once considered. Pumpkin could simply go to the door, shout, "Ding dong, Avon calling," and wait for Violet to open the door. A lightning fast nose-grab, and *voilà*, the perfect, bloodless *coup d'état*—or perhaps, *coup d'womb*.

Who could fault me if a small grin appeared as I imagined lapping the cream from a bowl of admiration offered by Wyatt, Shy Clayton and Metcalf? And yet, that brings to mind the words of wise old Ibid, "Pride goeth before destruction and then your ass is grass."

In truth, my three owl friends and I had made little progress in our plan to recapture The Old Home Place. Metcalf insisted that every fighting group must be known by an acronym. After hours of debate we voted to go with Shy Clayton's suggestion of "IHOP" (Invading Harry's Old Place).

Filled with sparkling enthusiasm for what I was now calling "The Pumpkin Plan," I asked Wyatt to assemble Shy Clayton and Metcalf for a council of war. With my warning that this was top secret stuff, they arranged my blanket over the crib in such a way as to create an almost impregnable War Room.

It was likely due the fact that none of these three had had their noses grabbed by Pumpkin, but my plan was received with an embarrassed, almost palpable silence. Had I suggested the use of dynamos, steam locomotives or chain saws, I believe it would have garnered a hearty reception. But a *nose grab?*

Metcalf was the first to speak: "Ahem. In the first place, and perhaps the only place, octopuses do not have noses. I therefore suggest that your suggestion is null and void."

Shy Clayton paled. "Are you suggesting that octopuses actually do not have noses?"

Metcalf raised his left eyebrow in semi-umbrage. It was insufficient for the task at hand. He added a raised right eyebrow, just a bit, announcing his intent to commit *full*-umbrage if required. "Please understand," he said, "you will not find one damn nose in a whole carload of octopuses!"

Shy Clayton, with an innate antipathy for umbrages in both the semi and full manifestations, sniffed politely, "I was only asking."

The news came as a stunning blow to me. Holy cow, no nose? Just leave it to an octopus to screw up the simplest plan! As Robert Burns might have said, my best laid scheme had "gang agley."

"What Ho? Harry boy?" Wyatt asked. He was always sensitive to my moods, "You look a little agley around the gills. Maybe you should wet yourself. That always cheers you up."

Metcalf pondered, looking pisster by the minute. "It's just a shame," he said. "All of those tentacles, the richest nose-picking potential in the world, and not a nose in a carload."

Shy Clayton, near tears, quoted his mother: "Eat your broccoli. Remember all those young octopuses in China have no noses to pick."

Even at that early time of my life I had noticed that epiphanies, like the leaves on poison ivy, come in threes. I closed my eyes and prayed. "Heavenly Father, please send me one more epiphany, and make it a damn good one because I'm in a bit of a bind. Just keep the last one for yourself or give it to your favorite charity. Best regards, Harry.

"P.S. I will hold my breath until I get this, even if I turn blue. I am serious. H."

I was epiphanized immediately, as was right and proper.

"Ok, boys," I cried. "Listen up. We have an epiphany here!"

Metcalf turned to Shy Clayton and shook his head. "How in the *hell* does he do that? I have never in my whole life received an epiphany without waiting at least six weeks."

Shy Clayton laid his wing on Metcalf's shoulder and said, "There, there."

I ignored Metcalf's jealous snit.

Proudly, I revealed my plan. "Now here's the way it will work: As near as I can tell, Pumpkin is not exactly the sharpest trowel in the potting shed. All I need to do is convince her that Violet's tentacles are noses. I could tell her the proper, scientific name is *Octopusium ad noseium*. She'll go wild! The only problem we'll have will be in holding her back."

There was a loud clapping of wings, and I believe I heard some silly talk of having a medal struck for me.

Well, of course it *was* silly, and yet...

13

I woke next morning knowing two things: the first, I was dying. The second, anyone stupid enough to live in a place like this rather than in a warm womb must be out of his rabbit-assed mind. My gums were chattering, and someone had packed my usually warm, wet diaper with ice cubes.

Grandmother Area Code 512 appeared in a fleece-lined bathrobe, her hair a disagreement between riot and pandemonium with mayhem struggling for a toehold. She wore custom-made Tony Lama cowboy boot bedroom slippers that included annexes for the accommodation of her bunions. The gentlest soul in the world would have to admit that when Santa Anna was butchering Grandmother's ancestors at the Alamo, he lost interest one ancestor too soon. She cantered past my crib taking the Lords' name *very* in vain and slammed shut the open window. "Ke-ke-ke-Keerist, it's cold."

She stomped out, casting not a glance at my pitiful, shivering gosling flesh, leaving me with her unspoken but definite surety of *my* culpability for the cold, damn-Yankee weather. A miasmatic blanket of guilt hovered above my crib, but brought no warmth. I wet myself—and discovered that a good piss likely brings more warmth and comfort than absolution.

By noon the frost was gone from the air. I had just finished nursing and barely started to spit up down the back of Mother's dress when the doorbell rang. Please, God, let it be Sweet Little Girl.

My visitor was Pumpkin. My heart was mud.

I suppose I should not have been surprised. Being granted two epiphanies in what some seemed to consider a very short time might be enough to expect. But I figured heck, what's one more little favor to Him?

It may have been a warning against greed and hubris, but I preferred to think that prayer is one of those cases where one takes a number and waits one's turn. Of course I would need to ask Wyatt about that; I could only hope I wasn't in a line with all those little Chinese octopuses that were hoping for noses to pick.

"Do you remember Harry, Pumpkin?" her mother asked, placing her in my bed and in my space.

Pumpkin did. Her hands quickly moved to protect her belly in anticipation of another lesson in the New Guinea Hairy Owl dialect.

And I remembered her. Like a Frenchman trained in *savate*, my feet assumed a fighting stance. "Play nice now," we were admonished. And we were left alone to choose friendship or Armageddon.

Knowing I had an important mission to accomplish, I quickly disarmed her with my sexy, toothless grin, and set out to teach her the Human words of "Ding dong, Avon calling." In half an hour, she could spout it out with the best of them. I then explained the anatomical anomalies of the octopus. "What at first glance appear to be tentacles," I lied, "are in actuality, noses. The greatest pleasure for an octopus is to have one of them grabbed and pulled until said octopus is out through the exit. And don't be alarmed if she seems to resist. Octopuses like to appear coy."

When the Mother Pumpkin bent to retrieve her darling, she was greeted by a loud and well enunciated, "Ding dong, Avon calling." Mrs. Pumpkin rolled her eyes to heaven, and exasperated: "Oh, Lord, what now?"

I just raised my eyebrows and tried to look as surprised as an orphan receiving a Hershey Bar.

With Pumpkin gone, I lay back and considered my good fortune.

Just picture me, Harry, the owl-faced boy, knowing that soon I would reclaim the womb—The Old Home Place! My invading cadre was complete, my ducks in a row, my new sharp arrow of vengeance and justice securely tucked in my quiver. Only the passage of time stood in my way—for Pumpkin and I must first learn to walk.

But then a dismal and surprising realization hit me. My always-reliable "deep memory" failed me. I was no longer exactly sure of the location of The Old Home Place.

So quickly and unexpectedly had my birth occurred, so brutally had I been grabbed, scissored and slashed that, in truth, there was little time to observe the local flora and fauna. I had given no thought to leaving a trail of breadcrumbs to follow back. The inside of the womb was forever in my mind, but I had neither time nor reason to glance at the exterior. Was it stone? Brick? Clapboard, or covered with asbestos shingles? Was it surrounded by a grassy meadow or tucked in a wooded glen? Was there at least a house number? Was there, perhaps, a mailbox with a little sign saying "Harry/Bitch Octopus Violet?"

My best hope was to talk to Wyatt. I had long suspected he knew more about me than he was sharing.

14

When Dung Beetle found that Grandmother Area Code 512 turned the thermostat to 85 degrees during the cold snap, he delicately bent the little pointy hand to read 85 when it was actually at 65. Grandmother told Dung Beetle there was something wrong with the damn thermostat, and she was freezing, and Dung Beetle told Grandmother there was something wrong with *her* damn thermostat, and that if she was freezing why didn't she burn her damn guitar? Whereupon, Grandmother told him that if he touched her new guitar she would break his damn collarbone again.

Is it any wonder I became depressed? From all indications, I would be expected to grow up using a language that had only one adjective to describe such exciting words as thermostat and collarbone. Would I be shunned by my peers if I escaped the boundaries of adjectical propriety and was heard to murmur something like: "Something's wrong with that flamboyant thermostat," or "I will break your ever-popular collarbone!" One would not last twenty minutes as an owl using only a *damn* this or a *damn* that.

Why, in High Owl alone one may find eighteen descriptive words for thermostat and the collarbone is always such a hot topic that new words are added every day.

In fairness to the Human tongue I must mention that in New-Guinea-Hairy-Owl-speak, there is *no* word for thermostat. Well, there is, but no one is allowed to use it. The King, who was a grumpy old gentleman at best, grew tired of everyone fiddling with his thermostat and declared the word taboo. Now, if you'd like the heat raised, you just incline your head toward the appropriate wall and say, "Would you mind turning the *you know* up a bit?"

A nearly extinct group of owls living close by the New Guinea Hairy Owl, and speaking the same dialect, have four hundred and nine words for describing the collarbone. They believe the collarbone to be a sex organ. So, as I said, they are nearly extinct.

I badly needed to talk with Wyatt, but as I lay there staring at the window, it occurred to me the window was closed. And for pity sake, the window was Wyatt's only means of entry and exit. I might never see him again! Devastated, I bawled and put up such a ruckus that I probably should have been keelhauled. But at that time Dr. Spock was still against keelhauling any children except teenagers.

Oh, me of little faith. How could I have ever presumed to doubt my godfather? He must have heard my caterwauling, for in minutes he swooshed blithely *through the closed window* and perched, Lombardy poplar toothpick securely in place, on the foot of my crib.

"How did you do that?" I demanded. Wyatt only winked.

"I'm an owl!" he replied, and seemed to be waiting for a trumpet fanfare.

"Do it again," I begged.

Wyatt welcomed my challenge and flew like a rocket toward the closed window and certain disaster. But there was no disaster, there was no crashing of glass, there was no dead owl bleeding on the floor.

He zipped in and out of the window as if he were a needle mending a tear. I stared in amazement. Then, for a grand finale, he floated, lazily, on his back, into the house and alighted on my crib. "I am an owl," he repeated, and I offered no argument.

"Are you sure you don't want to give up this foolishness about becoming human and become an owl?"

I admitted that I had been giving it some thought.

I explained my disgust at the paucity of adjectives in the Human tongue, and confessed my envy of the ability to fly through closed windows. Had it not been for the unpleasant thought of having a feathery pubic area, I believe I would have signed the pledge right then, and become an owl.

When Wyatt resumed his normal breathing and removed the self-satisfied grin from his beak, I reluctantly, and with some embarrassment, admitted my great problem: I could no longer remember the exact location of The Old Home Place.

A skeptical frown replaced his smug grin, and I knew I was faced with another danged owl mystery. I would, most likely, need to swear the oath of secrecy, ride the goat of initiation and learn the secret handshake of owldom before I could attain enlightenment.

Wyatt removed a huge silver watch from beneath his wing and said, "Want to see my new watch?" That explained why he had been flying a little lopsided, but did not answer my question and I was not about to be seduced into a detour.

"Now wait," Wyatt slowly began. "Are you quite sure your *mother* would enjoy having a ticklish, feathery owl fluttering around in her womb?"

Forgetting myself, I gathered all my strength and shouted, in Human Speak, "**I am not an owl!**"

Hearing my mother rushing down the hall, Wyatt disappeared. She gently cradled me to her breast and said, "Why, dear little Harry, of course you're not an owl, you do *look* a little like an owl, but you are a real human boy. Why, if you were an owl you would grow feathers in your pubic area!"

Holy cow! She's my *mother*, for gosh sakes. How did she know?

15

Of all the beasts that roam the woods,
I'd rather be an owl.
I'd sit on top of the schoolhouse,
And hear the teacher growl.

— *Translated from the original Persian by Shy Clayton*

I lay there in the early morning, eyes closed, and let the beauty of that ancient poem soothe my thoughts. I was thinking about Wyatt. There was a lot to think about. Wyatt is a lot of owl.

If you should find yourself sitting in a tall tree on a dark night, you just might meet up with Wyatt. Don't expect him to look much different from other owls, although I believe he is. My deep memory makes me believe both owls and goats are of a higher, more mystical order in this world—although maybe not entirely *of* this world.

Goodness only knows what my life would be if I had a goat for a godfather. Not that I would mind personally, you understand, but I'm sure the goat would soon grow weary of jumping in and out of the window at all hours of the day and night. If Grandmother Area Code 512 caught it, she would likely brand it and claim it as her own. And I would not like to be seen on the streets with a branded godfather.

My deep memory also tells me that what I consider my "deep memory" is a gift from Wyatt, as is my owl-like face, my ability with languages and, I must admit, my uncanny intelligence.

Now Wyatt is as fine a godfather as a boy might ever hope for. But still, I had begun to suspect he was not being completely forthright with me. It started when I asked him about the exact location of The Old Home Place. He hemmed and hawed, seemed to clear his throat more than usual and wanted to talk about how nice it would be if I became an owl. Goodness knows it was tempting, and Wyatt assured me he would take care of all the paperwork. Add in the fact that being a human baby is surely the most boring job in the world and...well, I really needed to think on it.

Parents terribly underestimate a baby's need for excitement and amusement. I remembered Wyatt's tales of his happy time as an owlet when his parents bought him a Sears and Roebuck Stradivarius. Wyatt loved that Strad, and practiced diligently until one day his father unaccountably seemed to lose his love for music. And, while adding a few words to Wyatt's vocabulary, he smithereened the violin into toothpicks.

But there my serious musings concerning the boredom of being a human baby and the mysteries surrounding my godfather came to an abrupt end.

Grandmother Area Code 512 pained herself into my bedroom and began damning her bicuspid to the hottest fires of Hell. The fact that there was no reason to believe I would know a bicuspid from a lump of bituminous coal never crossed her mind.

As she often did, Grandmother began her lamentations by dangerously mixing blasphemy with her Texas understanding of piousness. "If our creator, bless His name, had my damn bicuspid and a feathery pubic area, we'd both be tickled."

Thrusting her bony finger into her mouth, she explained: "Iss dissa ri eer." Then, perhaps not convinced I would recognize it if we met again in a dim light, she removed her upper plate and held the grisly thing right before my eyes. In a terror-filled reaction of survival, I batted the gruesome threat from her hand, sent it skittering across the floor, and started to howl. With an unnerving clack, the denture came to rest against the leg of the chiffonier. Well, except for the offending bicuspid, which continued to bound away with the speed of an orphan escaping from a cruel environment where potato salad was never served.

Grandmother screeched out one of her favorite words, then repeated it three more times, thus leaving no doubt. Without questioning the why or the how that a tiny owl feather came to be lodged between the molars, she blew some of the dust from the disgusting plate and slipped it back into her mouth.

A stunned expression on her face, and the sound of exultation from the depth of her heart: "Harry, you've *done* it!" It was not the "Harry! *Now* you've done it!" I hear when I fear I am facing extinction, but rather the kind of, "Harry! You've *done* it!" I might hear were I to find the lost Ark of the Covenant.

The biscuspidal pain was gone, as was the boredom of my day. And a grateful Grandmother Area Code 512 rushed out to light a candle in honor of her grandson: Harry, the patron saint of oral surgeons.

I dozed. Grandmother Area Code 512 had just knocked a humbled bronze Sam Houston off his bronze horse and replaced him with such a fine representation of a bronze, "Harry, The Oral Surgeon," that a "wanna be" sculptor like Michelangelo would have hidden his face in envy. A clever arrangement had been attached by which my diaper was constantly dampened, thus freeing the dedicated surgeon from the need to stop and stare in innocence at the wall while doing his business.

With my sharp and trusty little…(you know, one of those things oral surgeons use) I was about to put *finis* to an insolent and recalcitrant incisor when I was jarred awake by the door chime.

Even as I struggled to regain my moment of glory, I was recalled to the real world by joyous and happy laughter. Oh, far, far better than being haled as a hero! I was blessed with a visit from Sweet Little Girl.

The black clouds were rolled away and the sun brightened. It shown like a golden orb. The seas calmed and the waves caressed the shores with the promise of eternal love. The wolf lay down in peace with the lamb. Sweet Little Girl was laid beside me, and we were so filled with happiness that we joined hands and wet ourselves.

The problem of communication was still with us, but she had picked up a few words of Human, and, with little prompting, remembered many words I had taught her in High Owl Speak. By voice and sign, I asked her how the scab on her tummy button was healing.

"Oh, it's fine," she said.

I gave her my most innocent oh-gosh-and-by-golly-my-goodness grin and said, "I'd sure like to see it."

"Oh, you men are all alike," she blushed. "All you think about is a girl's tummy button." (But she showed me anyway, and this time I got a good look at it.)

Then, before I could wipe the sweat from my brow, she had us comparing toenails. A bold and forward girl, indeed, and I knew I was far out of my depth.

Love seems to be full of, "and thens," because and then—right in front of me, without the slightest sign of embarrassment—Sweet Little Girl began sucking her toe.

"Oh, Lord," I blurted, and gasped for oxygen. It was not exactly a prayer blurt, but it most certainly was not meant as a blasphemous blurt. It was simply the only sensible blurt to use when seeing a beautiful girl suck her toe.

"Oh," I begged, "I'd die for a chance to do that!"

"Well," the sly little minx replied, "you've got ten of them too, go ahead!"

But I was too far gone to play silly games. Without asking her consent or giving the promise of marriage, I seized her toe and sucked ravenously.

I was awash in the most ecstatic and blissful experience of which any man could ever dream. I was floating. I was drowning. I was the earth. I was the sky. My mind was a palette of the brightest colors, all jumbled with diamonds and shooting stars.

And then, it was time for another "and then."

And then Grandmother Area Code 512 walked in. "What in the name of our sweet, loving Lord Sam Houston is a goin' on here?"

She screamed. "Animals!" she screamed. She grabbed a full glass of water from the nightstand and drenched us. We each scrambled for our own sides of the crib looking guilty as hell. And, guilty we were.

My Mother and Sweet Little Girl's mother rushed in expecting and preparing for the worst. And that's what they found. Grandmother Area Code 512's nose was high in the air and emitting the smoke of righteous umbrage. "Toe sucking!" She screeched. "He was toe sucking! What kind of a son are you raising? A Frenchman? I'm not in the least surprised," Grandmother Area sputtered. "He likely learned it from his father. Genes will tell every time."

Sweet Little Girl and I faced each other like two hand-carved ivory cherubim, eyebrows raised in questioning innocence, *"Toe sucking?"*

Grandmother began what appeared to be a somber, perhaps ritualistic, flounce around the room, quoting scripture as fast as she could make it up. Her cadence could be counted by the repetition of the words "toe sucking."

"Just read your Bible," she exhorted. "Just look at the book of Genesis, it's so full of begets that you can't open a cold beer without first brushing away a whole passel of begets. And what *begets* begets? Why, it is toe sucking, my friends, pure and simple toe sucking! Y'all remember what happened to old Lot's wife? She doddled along, looking back over her shoulder for someone to suck her toes, and God turned her into a pile of iodized salt. If y'all don't change your ways around here and rid yourselves of your heathen behavior, we're all going to end up being a family of iniquitous damn salt shakers!

"And I'll warn you," she said pointedly, "We're not talking *low sodium* here."

Grandmother Area Code 512 marched out, head held high, leaving us with a faint odor of sulfur and a reminder that "toe sucking" and "tickling" were carved on the milestones to Sodom and Gomorrah.

Sweet Little Girl's mother bundled her up and they were gone. Alone again, I closed my eyes once more and happily envisioned my graven headstone. It was a tall, black marble obelisk, and the graven words read:

HERE LIES WICKED HARRY

The grinning wretch who lies below
Met his maker while sucking a toe.
Ye gentle virgins heed my song
And leave your little booties on.
For many a maiden's come to woe
By letting some bastard suck her toe.

16

Just as I felt I was getting a grasp on Human Speak, my father decided to reverse, as one might say, my educational polarity. In my sweetest voice, I asked "Da da" if we might go for a ride in the "car car." My aim, of course, was to visit Sweet Little Girl.

"It's not really 'Da da,'" he told me. "And it's not really 'car car.' Think singular. One. One car."

"Fair enough, Da," I replied, grasping the concept immediately. "Then I must also be wrong about the word 'brassiere.' There are two, now that I think about it. That's plural, two. Brassiere brassiere."

"NO!" He exasperated, turning a pleasing shade of pink, "It's *one* brassiere."

"Forgive me, Father, but with all due love and respect, and having been closely associated with 'brassiere brassieres' all of my life, I must disagree. We live in a world of balance. An unplural 'brassiere brassiere' simply would not fit in at all, and depluraled, (thus, 'brassiere') would be a freak for which you couldn't get a penny at a garage sale.

"There must be a left brassiere and a right brassiere. Now, it stands to reason that if only one brassiere had been needed, that *need* would be located in the center, and the balance and esthetics would be neat, tidy, and in harmony with the world, thus…"

Father roared: "Damn blam it, Harry, get this through your head. Two cups equal one 'brassiere!'"

Grandmother, coming in and catching only the last few words, roared: "Dung Beetle, you are, without a doubt, the dumbest man in the world. Even an idiot knows that two cups equal a *pint*! What you are teaching this child goes against God's plan and the wishes of the founding fathers of the Bureau of Weights and Measures."

When Sweetheart came in and announced my "din-din" time, I was vindicated. There were indeed two of them. And it bothered me not a whit whether I took my nourishment plural or singular, or from a pint or a furlong—there were two of them.

As Mother presented a most elegant arrangement for my luncheon pleasure, the dispute between Dung Beetle and Grandmother Area Code 512 raged on in the living room. Grandmother assuring the world that for thousands of years Dung Beetle's ancestors had lopped off their opposing thumbs saying, "The darn things just seem to get in the way." Dung Beetle, for his part, while not exactly denying her claim, maintained that Grandmother 512 had once paid three hundred dollars for a personally autographed photo of Jesus Christ, and another three hundred for three of the billfold size.

In the meantime, I enjoyed a leisurely "din-din" and pondered the scientific, social and economic ramifications of cross breeding a Maidenform brassiere with a hectare.

Well, as my god owlcle, Metcalf, likes to remind me, "Truth is stranger than Polish sausage." And when I had finished eating, my mother's first suggestion was a visit to Sweet Little Girl.

I signified my enthusiasm and the advancement of my vocabulary by shouting, "Auto auto," and by spitting up down the back of her sheer organdy blouse, where it was absorbed by her new dotted Swiss camisole.

Our trip to Sweet Little Girl's home was short and pleasant, enhanced by the sighting of several policemen, which according to Dung Beetle's sincere belief, proved that we didn't need one.

This was my first visit to Sweet Little Girl's bedroom, and I found it as lively and jolly as the annual horseshoe tournament given by

The Recumbent Order of the Owls. It was far different from my own, which boasted only a huge reproduction of Picasso's *Gurenica*. Dung Beetle received it as a replacement for the "girlie" calendar from Al's Automotive Repair Shop that Sweetheart considered vulgar and degrading to women.

Her crib was festooned with cheerful red, white and blue bunting that seemed to convey a subliminal message that here, indeed, was a perfect little firecracker. Suspended from the ceiling were smiling, cloud-like dinosaur mobiles with sleepy eyes, either unaware of their impending extinction, or (as with so many dinosaurs) just not giving a damn.

Wooly lambs and glistening lollipops, butterflies and ice-cream cones gamboled tirelessly across the wallpaper and around the room. There may have been the sound of a gentle waterfall. There may have been the silky, soft sound of a blossom entering full bloom. And…there may have been Pan, the god of those things our parents think we are too young to know about, breathing a licentious melody into his magic pipes.

Sweet Little Girl was resplendent: dressed in swirls of frills and pleats and bows—a veritable baby Rapunzel—but without all that damn yucky hair. Her eyes made the sun redundant. A dewdrop of nose-nectar twinkled, refusing to leave the tip of her nose, and the blood rushed to my head.

At the sight of me, Sweet Little Girl's Mona Lisa smile erupted into a somewhat coarse, Rabelaisian cackle. Placed beside her, I shivered.

My restraint was magnificent. The word "toes" did not cross my lips nor did my eyes wander low and betray my thoughts, my wishes. We spoke of the weather, the falling leaves, which were a new experience for both. And at length she offered me a taste of her "pacifier" and demonstrated how to use it.

I found the pacifier to be amazingly toe-like and therefore erotic. Still, when I tried it, I found a sense of dissatisfaction, a feeling of selfish self-gratification, a feeling of, "better than nothing…but…"

As I struggled to enjoy the toy, Sweet Little Girl kindly sought to lessen my embarrassment by telling me the history of the pacifier: "The first pacifier was a bone," she explained. "It was given to Cain and Abel and intended to be shared—to pacify those obnoxious brats. But Cain was strong as Aunt Edith's breath, and not really the shiniest hubcap in the parking lot. Abel was nothing but a selfish pie-hog. So, ironically," she said, quietly appreciating her own wit, "it became a bone of contention (her pun, not mine) and I guess you know the rest of the story."

Having built up a good head of steam by this time, I could wait no longer. I grabbed her foot, only to discover she was wearing tiny little shoes, and both were secured by what could only be Gordian knots. In frustration, I resorted to the first word I had learned in Human. "Brassiere brassiere!" I screamed.

Offended by my outburst, or what she perceived to be my ignorance, she corrected me. "Brassiere is one word. Singular. One!"

"Damn blam it," I roared. "What is the matter with you people?"

It was our first quarrel and I choose to believe, as first quarrels go, unique.

The feeling of guilt was new to me, undreamed of and certainly unwelcome.

The fact is, I would not have known the word "guilt" had not Wyatt found me gnashing my gums, wearing emotional sackcloth and thankful for the cigarette ashes Grandmother 512 accidentally dribbled onto my head.

"Guilt," he explained, "is when you have done something bad or wrong, and the thought of it makes you feel like a piece of doo doo."

Well, I was not about to become embroiled in another discussion of the plurality or singularity of words!

"Doo" or "doo doo," I didn't give a crap. But yes, I did feel like crap. I had quarreled with the only girl I ever loved.

"The problem is," Wyatt continued, "you are human. Humans are the only living creatures that feel guilt. Owls, for instance, never feel a twinge of guilt."

"Never?" I queried.

"Never," he replied.

"Not a twinge?" I pushed.

"Not a twinge," Wyatt guaranteed.

I could see it coming a mile away; it was going to be another "convert Harry to Owlism" day. Before he could slip his talons under his wing and bring out the legal paperwork for my signature, I held my hand up in the "wait" sign, just like the fat kid at the school crossing. "I need to enjoy this miserable, rotten feeling a little longer," I told him.

"Yep, it's lovesick guilt all right. The more it hurts, the better it feels. Just get over it, Harry. All you need to do is apologize. Admit it was your fault, beg forgiveness, and you'll be sucking toes before you know it."

"But, holy cow, Wyatt, it wasn't all my fault!"

"Fault, shmalt. Forget fault. The object here is peace in our time. You really don't know anything at all about women, do you?"

Wyatt started to leave, saying he would come back when I was feeling better. I told him I didn't want to feel better, I hadn't ask to be born and I wanted to die! I heard the word, "teenagers," and he was gone.

It was just as well. Sweetheart came in with my silver spoon and the green stuff.

I had been eating the green stuff for several weeks. The silver spoon was a gift from Grandmother Area Code 512. She said the big "DC" was Davy Crockett's monogram, but could not explain why the engraving also said "Souvenir of the Nation's Capital." At Grandmother's insistence I swore on my sacred honor to never divulge the fact that Davy Crockett's first name was "Washington." "What these Yankees don't know won't hurt them," she whispered. She claimed old Davy was eating green stuff with that spoon when he died at the Alamo.

I wasn't surprised.

Wyatt always maintained that the best food came wrapped in gray or brown fur, and the teeth, bones and toenails aided digestion.

At least I could depend on good old 512 for honesty. Sweetheart had tried to wean me from mother's milk by telling me the green stuff was green beans, the pinkish stuff was fruit and the brown stuff was beef.

Grandmother, watching out of the corner of her eye for the possible approach of the lying mother, whispered that in reality the green stuff was caterpillar *pâté*, the pinkish stuff was butterfly puke and the brown stuff was unicorn bile. From my deep memory, I knew anyone who loved me enough to give me so rare a gift as Davy Crockett's own personal spoon would never lead me astray about food.

Later, when I thanked her again for the spoon, she explained the reason the handle was a little bent. She said it was because Davy's antepenultimate act was to give a Mexican soldier a nasty cut just above the eyebrow. She paused and added, "After that Davy just rolled over, farted and died."

The green stuff seemed to act as a balm to my feeling of guilt, and I determined to take Wyatt's advice and apologize to Sweet Little Girl.

I remember this as being a hard day. Still, I had learned that a little green stuff and an apology will help fill the potholes on the road to love.

17

It was a few days later, in the early afternoon, when Wyatt again appeared. He was flying erratically and his eyes were a little glassy. Wyatt was high. Wyatt is the only one I know who can get high on the book of Isaiah. And he claims he doesn't have a problem! He says he only indulges when he's feeling low, but I know he also reads that passage when he is serious about pushing me down the path to Owldom.

According to Wyatt (and he regurgitated the essence of what he had just read), The Creator of All Things was in a bad mood. It was not His fault. Babylon had gone to hell and it looked to be cheaper to just destroy it and start over.

"Just what were those Babylonian rascals doing?" I asked innocently. "Didn't they take into consideration the loss of property values? Were they sucking toes?"

"Never mind," Wyatt blushed. "I'll tell you when you are older.

"The point is, Babylon was indeed destroyed, but here comes the good part, the *promise*." Wyatt could not quite suppress a sly grin as he quoted his friend, Isaiah: '*But wild beasts of the desert shall lie there; and their houses shall be full of doleful creatures; and owls shall dwell there, and satyrs shall dance there.*'

"I'll tell you for sure, when he heard the news of his new home, my ancestor, Phineus, was anything but doleful."

"Phineus?" I asked. "Was that really his name?"

"Not actually. His real name was Walt, but when he was almost personally mentioned in the Bible he felt that he needed a name with a little more panache than Walt.

"Now, don't interrupt. You see old Phineus was a very important owl. He was the first owl to fly. Until the Babylon thing came up, owls walked on the earth just like everybody else. But when The Creator of All Things told him to lie down and sleep with satyrs, old Phineus cocked his head and said 'Not me, Bubba, I ain't sleeping with no damn satyr. I know about satyrs.'

"Above all else, The Creator of All Things hated to be called Bubba, but he decided to let it pass, this once. 'OK, *Walt*,' The Creator said, knowing full well Phineus abhorred being called Walt, 'you can sleep in a bowling alley for all I care just as long as it's in Babylon. You can darn well sleep in a tree for all I care!' And to prove he was serious, He gave Phineus wings.

"So that was settled.

"Now, Harry, wouldn't you like to become an owl and join my long, illustrious lineage?"

"Wyatt, I've told you and told you, I'm too ticklish to have feathers growing in my pubic area. How about I just have feathers from my belt up?"

"Harry, a satyr is the only being who is part one animal and part another."

"So, maybe I'd rather be a satyr."

"No way! Satyrs have despicable habits!"

"Do they suck toes?"

"Most likely," Wyatt said, "but that's only the beginning of what they do."

"Let's cut to the chase, Wyatt. What else do they do?"

Wyatt skillfully ignored me as he was so often wont to do. "If you think feathers in your pubic area would bother you, then you could wear a codpiece."

"Wear a *codfish* in my pubic area?" I screamed.

"Not a codfish, you dolt," Wyatt sputtered, "a *codpiece!* Good

Lord, you put a dead codfish down there and an eagle would have it for breakfast before you could blink."

"Are you suggesting I might prefer a *live* codfish in my crotch? I think not!"

With a sigh, Wyatt's head drooped onto his breast. "I give up," he muttered.

There is no question in my mind, a boy could never have a better, more dedicated godfather than Wyatt. Still, sometimes I almost despaired of having a normal conversation with him.

It was not only Wyatt who tried to persuade me to forsake my human birthright. At times, both Shy Clayton and Metcalf had a go at it. Metcalf, for instance, once tried to ignite my enthusiasm with the tale of the tiny, forgotten nation called, "Little Ambivalent."

"It is," he said, "peopled entirely by owls."

"Are you sure the name was really 'Little Ambivalent?'" I questioned. "That seems like a strange thing to name a nation."

"Well,"... Metcalf was plainly making up his sales pitch as he went along. "These were strange owls. They couldn't make up their minds about anything. Some wanted to name their nation, 'Owloysius,' but others said that was the dumbest name they ever heard. Nobody in the world would ever be able to spell it.

"Another faction suggested, 'The Owl Kingdom of the Ocean.' But one bright young lad remembered that they had no ocean. 'All we gots is a little creek,' he said, 'and even I can piss across it.'

"And he proved it.

"So the name, 'Piss Creek' was kicked around for a while. But their spiritual leader, The Jolly Lama, declared that a nation with the word 'Creek' in it sounded puny, and without dignity.

"It wasn't until Mr. Randy McNally got around to inventing the world atlas that the place got its name.

"'What's this place called?' McNally asked, putting his pencil to his tongue.

"'We can't decide,' they told him.

"'A little ambivalent, eh?' McNally queried.

"'I don't know. I suppose so.'

"And that's what Mr. Randy McNally wrote: 'Little Ambivalent.'

"There was, however, one thing on which they could agree: the national symbol. 'It must be,' they said, 'an owl on the wing, an owl with an attitude. We want a haughty look on its face, and a vicious, writhing snake in its talons. And beneath the owl must be our national motto, *I Aint Takin' No Shit From Nobody!'*

"So they called in their most distinguished artist, and their most skillful tailor-craftsman, and together they created their national symbol.

"It was stitched of the finest gold and silver bullion thread, an elegant artifact. But while the artist and tailor-craftsman were their nation's best, in the eyes of the art world at large, these fellows might be found wanting.

"When the glorious national symbol was completed, the expression on the face of the owl looked, perhaps, a little more confused than haughty. Bewildered, one might say.

And the nationalistic sounding motto had been modified to read: *What the Hell Do I Do Now?*"

"Wait a minute, Metcalf." I interrupted, "What did these old Ambivalites eat?"

"Eat? *Eat?* How in the world would I know what they ate? For all I know, the little boogers ate…well…boogers!"

I could believe that.

"Did they have feathery crotches?" I persisted.

"Of course they had feathery crotches!" he miffed. "All owls have feathery crotches!"

"In truth, Metcalf, I'm not sure if you are trying to persuade me to *be* an owl, or *not* to be an owl. If fact, you seem, how shall I say this? A little…"

"I know," Metcalf sighed, "a little ambivalent."

18

Shy Clayton came alone—unusual, to be sure.

Came, with a very serious look on his face, reminding me of the time when Dung Beetle tried to explain to me how babies are made.

"It takes birds," he'd said, "birds and bees…and snails. Yes, I think snails are required. There, now, young Harry, any questions?"

I had none.

Father, aka Dung Beetle, patted me gratefully and hurriedly left my nursery believing he had successfully fulfilled a paternal, even sacred, obligation.

Unlike Dung Beetle, however, Shy Clayton showed no signs of being nervous. He settled himself comfortably, and spoke avuncularly. "Harry, I wonder if you have ever given any thought to becoming an owl. You are quite qualified, you know."

Well now, I said to myself, it's just pretty damn hard to think about anything else around here!

He spoke of the advantages, the privilege, of being an owl.

To Shy Clayton, Owlism was a calling, a Holy Order. With rising passion, his eyes became glowing embers of beatific, unquestioning fervency. To Shy Clayton, the word "Owl" was synonymous with, "above all else"—above the animal kingdom, above every creature that flies, above the pitiful, seething masses of mankind—more important than anything.

"Our German cousins have a phrase for it," Shy Clayton chuckled, "*Eulenhaft über alles*." And Shy Clayton stressed exclusivity: the secret wingshake, the cryptic words of recognition, and, (although only hinted at) the occasional masked ball.

Indeed, had I been of the Eskimo persuasion, and had Shy Clayton knocked at my igloo door offering me a better way to preserve my whale blubber, I would have bought a refrigerator on the spot. But, intuitively, I realized I was entering a danger zone. Unlike Wyatt, with whom I could speak frankly without giving offense, or Metcalf, over whom I could verbally run with a "car car" or verbally bulldoze aside with a "bulldozer bulldozer," Shy Clayton's delicate nature, his innate emotional gentility, could easily be crushed. I would, metaphorically, be treading on the owl-eggshells of his essence. I must reject his kind offer as gently as a mother butterfly might touch her little papoose-pupa.

Although his eloquence all but demanded acceptance of his proposal, I knew I must decline.

"Shy Clayton, my dear friend, your words have touched my heart. To live as an owl must surely be the grandest life in the world, but alas, I am unworthy."

"Unworthy? Ridiculous!" Shy Clayton laughingly assured me. "You are the very embodiment of all the qualities we seek in an aspirant."

"I'm unworthy!"

"You are not!"

"Really, Shy Clayton, I'm just a shithead."

"No! You are a perfect fit for Owlism!"

"Am not!"

"Are too!"

"I would simply detest having feathers in my pubic area!"

"You'll get used to them."

"Will not!"

"Will too!"

"I hate owls!"

"You, Sir, are a walking affront to every owl!"

"Well, *Sir*, I say screw every owl and the horse they rode up on!"

"Owls don't ride horses. I should know, I'm an owl!

"You can say that again!"

"I don't chew my cud twice, and you *are* a shithead!"

"Ditto."

"Right back to you with a double ditto."

"Ha!"

"I'll take that, "Ha," as an agreement to my statement!"

"And I'll tell you where you can stick your statement too!"

"Harry, if you ever, ever, ever, try to become an owl, I swear I will blackball you!"

"And I'll tell you what you can do with your balls, be they black, blue, or the colors of a desert sunset!"

Shy Clayton left in a grand huff, but not before flipping me the middle feather of his wing. I believe that was the only time I've been flipped the bird *by* a bird.

19

As I approached my eighth month in this strange but rather pleasant life, I often found myself thinking back to the old days. Surely those first days were terrifying. I cringed at every approaching footstep, fearing the slice of another knife, the snip of another scissors.

As the early days passed, however, my parents appeared satisfied with what was left of me, and the mutilation stopped.

From my deep memory, I knew humans are sometimes enthralled by the so-called art of topiary, so I formed the habit of examining my body daily for new runners, shoots or branches that might call for additional pruning. I could only say, so far, so good.

What with my humans, my godfather, Wyatt, and my owlcles, I rarely wanted for company.

Sweetheart, the mother, continued to provide a veritable artist's palate of food. I will admit that at first I found these bright colors distasteful; after all, I was used to pure white mother's milk, but on examining the results of my spit up, I found the colors delightful. When Mother found it somewhat less than delightful, good old Dung Beetle reminded her that Jackson Pollock got his start in exactly the same way. Though usually supportive of my artistic endeavors, she still adamantly refused to display her artistically enhanced blouses on the refrigerator door.

As for Dung Beetle, his visits continued, as did his efforts to improve my vocabulary. I told myself that as I grew older, such words as "polyurethane," "escarpment," and "poltergeist" would be of great value to me, although I sincerely doubted I would ever find any word as all-round useful as "brassiere brassiere."

After living with this family for eight months, I concluded that even with my owl-like tendencies I was the most normal one. Only my love and my generous nature allowed me to describe Sweetheart and Dung Beetle as merely eccentric. Grandmother Area Code 512 was simply as loopy as a bowl of spaghetti. She was, and still is. She also has rocks in her head: igneous, metamorphic and sedimentary.

Given a choice, I believe Grandmother Area would have preferred a Hereford calf rather than a somewhat-owl as a grandson. Still, she does the best she can and works to improve my education. I knew she had accepted me when she started daily readings of *The Geological Survey of Travis County, Texas, Vol. One.* It's a fascinating picture book showing each rock in her home county. Grandmother, of course, has her favorites. "Looky here," she will say. "This one's just a tiny little ol' thing!" Or perhaps, "Would you just look at this! He's a whopper! A real Texan!" To date I have a nodding acquaintance with 4,362 rocks.

My first impression of Wyatt was quite wrong—well, my second, actually. My *first* impression comes from my deep memory. Wyatt flying in circles above an old Chevy, distracting my mother from the serious business of conceiving me. Distracting her in a way I'm now convinced...but no, " impressing" is a more accurate word. Impressing her. And at the instant of bliss she was seeing *his* face. The result? I was born with a face very much like that of an owl.

I suppose I really shouldn't have been watching, but I mean, gee whiz!

I can't say I was surprised to find I had an owl for a godfather. For all I knew Owl godfathers were standard issue in my new world. For gosh sakes, after having my only means of support snipped off and my tallywhacker whacked, why should a little thing like an owl godfather bother me?

Now try to stay with me on this—sometimes my life before birth and my life after birth seem to run together. Thus, you may see, I am now talking about my *second* impression of Wyatt, but my *first* impression after my birth. To me he appeared scruffy at best; down at the heels. He had a sort of second-hand look about him—yes, a *used* owl.

But knowing Wyatt has been an important lesson for me, I have learned that *one can't judge an owl by his feathers.* (I must make note of that line and use it in my autobiography.)

The fact is, Wyatt may well have been more surprised than I to find himself cast in a god-fatherly role.

He gets full marks, however. In a very short time he pulled himself together, properly preened, and made every effort to fulfill his god-fatherly obligations.

And surely no one can fault Wyatt in regard to my education. Early on he concluded that given a pencil, I would likely put my eye out with it, and therefore, my learning must be achieved through memory. He was determined that I receive a well-rounded education, and lectured me on history, literature, language and all things pertaining to life.

From time to time, both Shy Clayton and Metcalf appeared as guest lecturers. Shy Clayton tutored me in music and the arts. And the down-to-earth Metcalf filled my mind with such things as economics, foreign and domestic policy and pool hall etiquette.

Of course, both as a group and individually, they monitored my love life and made the most useful suggestions.

Together with Shy Clayton and Metcalf, my god owlcles, Wyatt pushes me ever nearer to resigning my commission as a human and joining the happy ranks as a volunteer owl.

Grandmother Area Code 512 also contributed to my education. Sometimes, for the delicious deviltry of it, she would bring in a long-necked beer, adrip with icy moisture. She'd quickly check the dark corners of my room. Surreptitiously dip two fingers into her cleavage and pull out a nipple! Not the whole breast as Mother might, just the nipple. I had never considered that the damn things might be detachable, but I suppose they do have to be washed and dried and, perhaps, polished. As Wyatt says, there's a lot I don't know about women.

At any rate, she deftly slipped that nipple over the mouth of the long-necked beer bottle and placed it to my mouth.

At first, the nipple had a bit of a rubbery taste to it and I chalked that up to Grandmother's age, but as the nectar gurgled down my throat that taste was easy to ignore. Oddly enough, the ache in my heart for The Old Home Place seemed to lessen with each swallow. In truth, perhaps my New World might not be so bad.

20

At eight months, I was rarely receiving telepathic messages from my twin sister, Violet, the bitch octopus. The reception seemed to grow weaker each day, and often there were strange, grunting noises as if she were straining to be heard at all. Sometimes only heavy breathing came into my mind, other times there was a soft giggle and a pitifully disguised voice asking if I had Prince Albert in a can. Obviously Violet had been hitting the old umbilical cord during the cocktail hour.

I hated it when she teased me about The Old Home Place. "The abdomen is lovely this time of year," she would say. "The industrial sound of the grinding colon, the soft gurgling of the urinary tract. Why, sometimes I can even hear the sad singing of the workers in the far away follicle fields. '...I'm coming, for my head is bending low.' I swear, Soggy Butt, sometimes its so nice I just feel like crying."

Ah ha, I thought, she knows my nickname and uses it cruelly. A tricky one, she has planted a spy in my midst, and I didn't even know I had a midst. It did no good to turn off my receiver, she just kept pushing the telepathic redial button until we connected. To make her jealous of my life as a human I told her of my learning about the rocks of Travis County, Texas. She impaled me with a telepathic sneer. I concentrated on wishing her an ugly wart where it hurts when she sits.

I was damning "twin-telepathy" to high heaven when Wyatt, Shy Clayton and Metcalf silently coasted in and alit on the foot rail of my crib. Metcalf raised a warning wing to still my blasphemy. He quickly pulled a blanket over my crib so God couldn't hear, and all three crowded under. "It was God's nephew, Archie, who invented telepathy," he whispered, "And if you don't want your pecker to become a lightning rod, you'd better cool it." Shy Clayton covered the embarrassment caused by that word by covering his beak with the tip of his wing. Wyatt covered his ears with *his* wings. Owls hate thunder.

My deep memory reminded me that Benjamin Franklin invented the lightning rod, and I could but wonder if God had caught him blaspheming Archie's invention.

Be that as it may, I quickly redirected my thoughts to something less dangerous.

"The first thing I'll do when I retake The Old Home Place," I declared, "will be to smash Violet's telepathic transmitter."

Wyatt and my two god owlcles were taken aback. The feathers on Metcalf's brow furrowed in doubt, "I can't imagine an octopus without a transmitter," he admitted.

"Wouldn't be much of an octopus without a transmitter, I'll be bound!" Shy Clayton concurred.

"And still," Wyatt added thoughtfully, "Violet won't be much of an octopus when we are finished with her anyway."

Grandmother Area Code 512's footsteps came scruffling down the hallway, and the three owls bade me a hasty adieu.

Grandmother Area leaned her long-necked bottle against my belly as she changed my diaper. "Now in Texas, Harry, some of the old folks can read the future from the dregs in the bottom of their beer glass." Her eyes took on that far away, Texas look; I did not interrupt. She stared at my nakedness as if for the first time, "And in Texas," she mused, "I once knew a fellow who had been circumcised with a pair of pinking shears."

"Was he a nice man?" I inquired.

"He was…interesting," she replied thoughtfully, and she nodded her head in agreement. "Interesting."

21

Pumpkin returned to my life with the unearthly smell of ozone and the sound of God's first practice clap of thunder, which even He had admitted was a little too loud. She arrived, as she reckoned was her right, her privilege.

She had grown since her last visit. Now larger than I—to use the word "plump" would be a kindness. Still with no teeth, for which I gave thanks; she would surely be a biter. Her hair was longer, denser and, of course, still red. It was not the red so often described as "flaming red," but rather the red of an ember, an ember eager at the first breath of air to burst into flame. In point of fact, Pumpkin seemed to carry the threat of bursting into flame herself, a flame that would not consume *her*—but woe to the world around her.

A little intimidated, I asked, "So how has life been treating you, Pumpkin?"

"Don't call me 'Pumpkin,' Harry, I've outgrown that. My name is 'Lilith.'"

"That's fine, er, Lilith."

"Don't be condescending to *me!* 'Lilith' is just as good a name as 'Harry!'"

"It's probably better," I suggested.

"Damn right!" she said.

I decided to change the subject.

"Are you all ready to knock on the door of The Old Home Place and cry, 'Ding dong, Avon calling'?"

"I've been wanting to talk to you about that." She gave me a look so hostile that had I been a tobacco leaf I would have gone up in enough smoke to cause cancer in seven counties. "There's not going to be any of that 'Ding dong, Avon' crap! I have no intention of helping evict that poor female from her home!"

"*Her* home?" I cried. "It's *my* home, too, for gosh sakes! I'm the one who was evicted. I was *evacuated*, kicking and screaming, against my will! A classic case of premature evacuation!"

She sneered me a caustic, "You poor little man."

I flew into a rage. Then as quickly, I cringed into cowardice.

"We women will no longer be your slaves, your chattel, your toys, your conveniences, to be evicted at your whim!"

"Are you talking, like—equal pay for equal work?" I asked.

"Right on, Buster!"

Feeling that I might be on a roll, I suggested, "How about a stitch in time saves nine?"

"No way, José! No more mending and no more washing socks and underwear!"

"I suppose that includes diapers?"

She did not deign to answer.

"And what about Apple Pie and Motherhood," I queried.

"Oh, yes," she said, "there will still be Motherhood—just no fatherhood." Even as my mind began to see a potential problem there, Pumpkin pulled herself erect. Setting herself suddenly straight, with her shoulders back, she beat her little chest with her tiny fists and shouted, "**I am Lilith! I am Woman!**"

I soiled myself.

22

"Do you remember telling me that I knew nothing about women?"

"Of course," Wyatt replied.

"Well, as of today I know even less."

Wyatt smiled sadly. "You're learning," he said.

"I'm devastated," I replied. "Pumpkin, aka Lilith, was my brightest hope for reclaiming The Old Home Place. And now…and now, that sweet hope has been dashed asunder!"

"'Asunder' is a good word, Harry, remember it. You'll use it a lot in this life."

Those were not words I wanted to hear. Not for the first time, Wyatt sounded less than enthusiastic about my returning to The Old Home Place. Still, to be fair, if *my* Old Home Place were a claustrophobic egg, half filled with green baby owl doo doo….no, I couldn't blame him.

I pondered. "Is it really green?" I asked.

"Is what really green?"

"Baby owl doo doo!"

"What in the *hell* are you talking about?"

"Never mind, Wyatt. I just want a little commiseration here, a shoulder to cry on."

"Harry, there is nothing an owl hates more than having tear-besogged shoulders. Let me tell…"

"Stop trying to change the subject!"

"So," Wyatt said, "you still want to talk about green baby owl doo doo?"

"Wyatt," I cried, "I do not want to talk about green baby owl doo doo, and I do not want to talk about besogged owl shoulders!"

"Good. I'll go home and get some sleep."

"Wyatt, for Pete's sake, try to understand. I'm running out of time! I've been getting these telepathic messages from Violet. She's going to redecorate the place again. She's thinking about getting those little round-bottom, spindly-legged chairs like they use in ice cream parlors! First thing you know she'll be allowing parties and you won't be able to hear yourself think because everyone will be singing 'Happy Birthday to You.'"

Shy Clayton flew in, followed by Metcalf—who was licking his beak and saying, "Did I hear somebody mention birthday cake?"

Owls love birthday cake.

Through my frustration I tried to explain that Pumpkin had morphed into a Lilith and was refusing to say "Ding dong, Avon calling."

Shy Clayton's little eyebrow feathers shot up a half inch as he gasped out, "My soul!"

But if you think Shy Clayton's reaction was astonishing, you should have seen Metcalf's face turn red. "Just like a woman," he snorted. "You buy them gifts, sweet talk them, promise them the stupid moon, and then, when the time seems just right, you make that one little request. 'Oh, no,' they'll say, 'I promised my mother I would never say, "Ding dong, Avon calling," until I was married.' Doggoned women."

Wyatt lifted his wings as if to offer a benediction, and I hoped with all my heart he would.

"Wait, now. Everyone just wait. Harry, I hate to be the one to say this, but I fear your dreams of returning to The Old Home Place are in vain. Why, you don't even know where it is."

Metcalf was fit to be tied. "Do you mean to tell me they have hidden Harry's Old Home Place? Doggoned women!"

Shy Clayton extracted a small book from under his wing: *Familiar Quotations*. He scratched out one word and was writing above it: "For want of a 'Ding dong' a kingdom was lost." He closed the book quickly and tucked it away beneath his wing.

23

Grandmother Area Code walked into the room and my hand automatically dipped to the safety pins that guaranteed the preservation of my modesty. She laughed. She always laughed at that. "Racial memory," she swore. "The old 'Adam Syndrome,'" she called it. The subject seemed to fascinate her, perhaps even more than the rocks of Travis County, Texas.

"Old Adam did the same thing with his fig leaf, you know. Even if there was no one around but God. And it was God who had made him, for goodness sakes—it's not like He was going to see anything that might surprise Him! See, the first time Adam 'checked his fly,' as they call it now, it was simply because the damn thing itched. He was scratching. It wasn't modesty, I'll tell you. Modesty hadn't even been invented yet.

"Now this is just my own theory, my guess, if you want to call it that, but I think seeing Adam dip his hand down there that way just sort of tickled something in God.

He was probably ready for a good laugh anyway. So He just pushed a button or rang a bell for an angel, and said, 'Make a note of this, Charlie. Always check your fig leaf. Put that in the racial memory of Man.'

"Then, if I'm any judge of angels, old Charlie probably asked, 'What about the racial memory of Woman?'"

"And God would say, 'Just in case you haven't noticed, Charlie, there are no women.'

"So then, Charlie likely said something like, 'That's right! So why does Adam bother to wear that stupid fig leaf?'

'It's for protection. Adam claims it's a total bitch when that little thing gets sunburned,' God answered.

"So time went by and everything went pretty well for the most part. Sometimes Adam would check his fig leaf and sometimes he would forget. God didn't really make a big deal of it.

"But then, just as if the idea had been His all along, He created Woman.

"Now, she turned out to be Eve. And since things seemed to be going well for her, she didn't have much to complain about. Well, not until Adam told her about God's order concerning checking one's fig leaf.

"Now see, that was before Adam learned to keep his mouth shut. Anyway, Eve kept her eyes open and every time Adam forgot, Eve would say something smart, like, 'You better shut the barn door or your horse will get out.' And that just confused old Adam, because horses, like modesty, hadn't been invented yet.

"You understand now, Adam wasn't exactly the brightest flower in that Garden of Eden, but eventually he caught on. When his sons, Cain, Abel, and after a while, little Seth, came along, Adam, by God (pardon my French), would thonk them on the head with his knuckle if they forgot to close their flies. This is the truth now, he thonked them so often that they were half-afraid to pee. And it went on like that, from father to son and from father to son, until now the male of the species checks his fly without even knowing it.

"You just watch your father, old Dung Beetle, he checks his fly at least fifty times a day and I doubt he has that much to be modest about. And now you're doing it and I know you can't help yourself. Does your dad ever head-thunk you?"

"No, Ma'am," I told her.

"Well, you just go ahead and do it, and don't be embarrassed. It's God's will."

I guess nobody knows her Bible better than Grandmother Area Code 512.

Three days later, Sweet Little Girl blessed me with a visit. I was just finishing my lunch-suckle and, as God had commanded, I plunged my hand down for a quick check.

"Stop that!" Mother squealed. "That tickles!" Some things mothers just don't want to know. But God knew.

And Sweet Little Girl knew, too, though she never showed it. A part of Woman's racial memory is to pretend not to notice when a man checks his fly, and Sweet Little Girl, her blue eyes as innocent as an orphan's fart, pretended not to notice.

Having, without giving it a thought, paid our respects to God's will and racial memory, Sweet Little Girl and I melded into a cozy lump. Her breath was delicately redolent of what had become my favorite scent, Essence *de Spitup*. Asparagus *la Purée* might be noted, and sometimes, Grandiose *du Goop,* by Gerber, *avec Frère Jacques.* This girl has expensive taste, I'll be bound!

I waited as long as able, and then blurted the question I feared most but had to ask. "Your name is still 'Sweet Little Girl,' isn't it?"

She gently pushed me away, the better to see my face. "Why, of course it is, Harry, you silly thing."

I remembered Dung Beetle's lessons concerning avoirdupois when he had counseled me, "In for sixteen ounces, in for a pound."

I plunged ahead. "How do you feel about equal pay and washing underwear and socks?" So much depended on her answer!

"Harry, now stop, you're scaring me."

"Just promise me that you won't change your name to Lilith," I begged.

"Well, of course I won't. That's a stupid name."

Reassured, and at peace in my mind, I let my eyes stray boldly downward to her lovely toes. My eyes strayed hungrily and stared greedily. And the Word blazed before me, and the Word was **"toes**."

A soft, shy smile came to her lips, and her eyes offered me more promises than an Oklahoma faith healer.

24

Wyatt perched on the foot of my crib, his Lombardy poplar toothpick dangling from his beak. It drooped sadly, as might the tail of a vanishing luncheon-mouse.

Vanishing, as had Sweet Little Girl in the arms of her anguished mother who, seeing her sucked-bright red toes, had assumed the worst: Trench toe.

Had anyone bothered to notice, they would have seen that my lips were a bit puffy. But only Wyatt noticed, and only Wyatt knew the cause.

"Harry, Harry," he admonished, "You must curb this insatiable desire to suck Sweet Little Girl's toes."

"I just can't help myself," I replied, "I'm a sucker for toes." A line like that would have brought down the house in any venue in the country, but Wyatt never cracked a smile. He ignored my attempt at humor as steadfastly as one must ignore the Queen's fart.

"Be honest with me now, Wyatt. Don't owls ever, in the throes of passion, have the desire to suck a lady owl's toes—er, talons?"

Wyatt pulled his longest, sternest owl face and said, "Certainly not! There is an ancient owl legend that tells of a young owl that tried that very thing. The lady's foot slipped and her talon ripped through his carotid artery. Heed my words, young Harry, for the ancient wisdom can guide you in your future. In your youthful passion,

Sweet Little Girl's toes may be your fondest desire. But time passes. Sweet Little Girl, like all of us, will grow old. She will come to look like her mother, then her grandmother. Consider well, Harry, would you like to suck her grandmother's toes?"

The sound of my retching was lost in my grandmother's scream from the front door that may well become a legend itself. Terrified, Wyatt flew through the window leaving only a foggy trail of wisdom, morality and mortality behind.

The chime of the doorbell had not reached my mind as I visualized Sweet Little Girl's grandmother's feet with corns, bunions, calluses and yellowed toenails. But that gentle sound was the sound of sadness, and death entered our house.

The telegram was for Grandmother Area Code 512, and it told of the coming suicide of her ex-husband, Billy Area Code 512. Grandmother had kept her married name.

As Grandmother later explained it to me: "Billy was never one to rush things. He was the slowest, most procrastinating man that ever lived, and that's why I left him. Still, I guess I must have loved him at one time, and it pains me to think of him down there slowly committing suicide all alone."

So there it was—not yet one year old and I must learn about death. My own ex-step grandfather had planted a small pecan tree in his backyard, brought out a chrome and plastic chair from the kitchen, tied one end of a rope around a branch, and the other around his neck. With a pitiful cry of, "Goodbye, cruel world," he sat down to wait. Sat there, as Dung Beetle imagined, whittling on a dark piece of monotony.

In the meantime—much as King David mourned for his son, Absalom—so mourned Grandmother Area Code 512 for her Billy. Her only solace being that in about twenty-two years, when the tree had grown threateningly tall, she would return to Texas and rescue his sorry butt.

It was well after lunch when Wyatt dared venture again to the foot of my crib. Owls hate morning mourning moaning.

All thoughts of my lust for toe sucking seemed gone from his mind, yet I wrestled with the problem. Was it mine alone?

Shy Clayton and Metcalf had come along shortly after Wyatt, so I turned to Shy Clayton, whose knowledge of world religions was great.

"Why is it," I inquired, "that thumb sucking is considered normal and even 'cute' for a baby, and toe sucking is viewed as an abomination?"

"I'm not sure." he admitted, "Maybe if you tried saying grace it would alleviate the stigma."

"I'm not *eating* her toes for Pete's sake, I'm just sucking them!"

"Yes… well, I think a good incantation might be in order here."

While Wyatt chafed in disapproval and Metcalf worried an annoying earwig, from beneath his wing Shy Clayton withdrew a sheet of foolscap, a quill pen, and a charming Lalique ink well.

In a fine Spencerian hand he composed his petition to Aphrodite, the goddess of love:

> Oh sweet Aphrodite please button your nightie
> And pray pay attention and listen to me.
> For I fear your attractions will cause me distractions,
> And I have enough problems for now, don't you see?
>
> With your Magic Girdle, please smooth out the hurdle
> Of social repugnance for our kind of lust,
> And allow us a measure of toe-sucking pleasure,
> We poor wretched mortals. In you lies our trust.
>
> Remove the restriction on our sweet addiction,
> Oh, grant us this favor. Bless us from above.
> And shut off the spigots that nourish the bigots
> Who deny us legitimate toe-sucking love.

Wyatt, as my godfather and protector, suffered a sudden guilt of righteousness and was incensed that my young ears heard the word "girdle."

Metcalf was incensed at Wyatt's incensocity and suggested he, "Get real. I suggest you stick to teaching the kid how to subjugate verbs, and let me handle his worldly education."

Shy Clayton, searching his rhyming dictionary for an alternative for "girdle," rejected "turtle" as a word that would only piss Aphrodite off—thus ending love and thus ending life on Earth as we know it.

Grudgingly, Wyatt admitted the necessity of the word "girdle," but tenaciously insisted that a rider be added to the petition, whereby the *suckee* assumed all responsibility for any injury to the *sucker's* carotid artery.

25

Truth to tell, the impending demise of my ex-step grandfather caused little disruption in the lives of Grandmother 512, Sweetheart, Dung Beetle and myself. The wailing and gnashing of teeth ended shortly after it began. Messages from Texas neighbors informed Grandmother that an umbrella had been provided for Billy, and food was being prepared for him daily. A license was granted to allow a fee to be charged to view the only living suicide in Texas, and a local newspaper quoted my ex-step grandfather as saying, "I never had it nearly this good when I was almost alive."

Grandmother Area Code reached the point of frothing at the mouth and swearing to sue his butt off for alimony. "Why should he be so happy while I'm crying my eyes out?" She swore if she lost at court she'd fertilize that damn pecan tree until it grew like a mad weed.

In the meantime, Metcalf had become completely enamored with Shy Clayton's incantation to Aphrodite. He committed it to memory and started changing some of the lyrics—a word here, a word there. I could almost hear the little wheels in his mind churning out notes, sharps, flats, rests and tremolos.

As my eyelids grew heavy, Wyatt and the two god owlcles tip-taloned to the window and silently flew away.

I dosed.

And as I dosed, I dreamed of toes.

Dreamed—hell, I *nightmared*. Toes, grandma octopus toes, scaly, painted-red nails, blistery, blustery, offering-no-quarter, throat-gagging grandmother octopus toes. They were green toes, mostly, but sometimes of an iridescent mother-of-pearl hue. My toes stay the same color the year around with never a sign of change, and I was appalled by that unfairness. You will find no fairness among octopus toes, my friend. They can be whatever color they choose. The bastards.

I woke from my nap gratefully, with the pleasantness of a brown, long-necked bottle chilling a wet circle on my tummy. Blessed art thou, Grandmother Area Code 512! In her own Grandmother-of-the-Year way, she gave me a long swig of beer, changed my diaper, and was gone.

Silent as an earwig's belch, Metcalf floated in followed by Shy Clayton and Wyatt.

Around his neck Metcalf sported a dogwood flower lei; in his talons he gentled what might have been a four stringed luncheon-bunny, but was, in fact, a ukulele.

Given the choice, most people would have chosen a bunny.

Perched on the foot of my crib, the three settled in. Metcalf, looking proud as a three-peckered goat, produced a felt-plectrum, and the thrums of old Hawaii were a balm to my octopus-toe scared heart.

As Shy Clayton stared pensively straight ahead, Metcalf sang his new words to Shy Clayton's incantation to Aphrodite:

"Oh my sweet wahine, untie your bikini…"

Metcalf's lyrics went quickly from raucous to worse. And yet, surprisingly, Shy Clayton's wing feathers fluttered hula-like, describing the gentle swaying of the palms, the beloved thrills and dangers of the sea, the smoky forgottenness of ancient volcanoes.

And Wyatt?

Why, Wyatt's little owl-hips rotated in racial memory from a time when owls danced on the sands of Waikiki.

"Holy H. Cow, Metcalf," I cried. "I had no idea you could play the ukulele!"

A feathery eyebrow raised just enough to admit a superior disdain.

"Well, Mr. Smarty Pants, answer me this: If an albatross can play a tenor banjo, why should not an owl play a ukulele?

In truth, I could not fault his logic.

26

On Tuesday afternoon, the inevitable—as inevitables are so often wont to do—happened. Pumpkin cum Lilith cum Curse-Of-My-Life, arrived for another visit. Our mothers had become best of friends. And thus, through God's questionable wisdom, were the sins of the mother (aka Sweetheart) visited upon the head of the son (aka me).

Flaunting a lapel pin with the words, "More Votes for Women," Lilith immediately established her dominance by staring me down.

In as non-aggressive a voice as one might ever hope for, I said, "It has been my understanding that women already have the vote."

"**The** vote, yes," she replied. "**The**, as in one; **the**, as in singular; **the**, as in not en-goddamn-ough!"

"En-*what?*"

"Enough. *enough*, **e-n—g-o-d-d-a-m—o-u-g-h!**"

"I see."

"Look, now, when a man dies his vote is gone, right?"

"Well…"

"Well me no wells. Am I right or am I right?"

"But the lucky widow almost always gets the house, the home."

"Big deal! So the pitiful widow inherits some old termite ridden house that should have been burned down years ago, while what she really needs is her late husband's vote."

"Are you telling me that my mother's uterine walls are being chewed up by termites? No way!"

"I'm telling you that what the poor woman really needs is the use of his vote."

"But what if she doesn't vote the way he would want?"

"He should have thought of that before he so dumbly died, shouldn't he?"

"Dumbly died?"

"Forget it. Is there anything to eat around here? You're not much of a host, are you?"

"Sometimes Grandmother Area Code 512 brings me a little peanut brittle, but you don't want to hear about that. Mother claimed it was petrified doo doo."

"And there you go again! Just like a man, keeping your secrets to yourselves. As a woman, I demand my rights. I demand to know the secret of petrified peanut brittle doo doo!"

"No offense, it's something nice people don't talk about."

"No offense? *No offense?* You, in essence, are saying that I'm not 'nice,' and it's no offense? You, in essence, are calling me a 'trailer-trash bitch,' and I should not be offended?"

It was then God's mercy became manifest. The mother of this little girl, aka *whatever*, came in and was greeted with: "Mother! I demand some petrified peanut brittle doo doo!"

What she got was a smart swat on her little pumpkinesque butt. And, in my opinion, it was about time too.

There really is a God, you know.

27

Father, aka Dung Beetle, swears it is a grievous crime to teach girls to read.

Grandmother Area swears Dung Beetle himself is a misdemeanor, and if he were any dumber he would be a felony.

Their arguments are ongoing and never ending. Had this one not concerned my mother, it would have just been "business as usual." But since my birth, it has been her habit to sit by my crib and read to me. Well and good, you may say, that's what Mothers are supposed to do. But she does not read me stories about fat little roly-poly piggies, nor yet about cuddly bears stealing honey. A good little hairy Christian spider out to save the world would be welcome. Oh, no, not *my* mother.

Child health and child development is her passion, and the stack of childcare books in the corner of my room grows…and grows. As she reads the advice in them she watches me, furtively as a Supreme Court Justice picking his nose. She watches for red spots and white spots, drab spots and sparkly spots; she checks for fever and she checks for chills. She reads and she checks. Her fear of diaper rash is the worst, for at the first sign of it I am packed—head to toe—in talcum powder.

"Diaper rash can spread like impetigo," she explains. She examines me from toe to eyebrow to the soft spot on the top of my head. Neither plague no pestilence, neither diphtheria nor diarrhea, brought forth such concern as did diaper rash.

There are days when I look as white as an "after the beheading" picture of Anne Boleyn, and Wyatt declares that I may be destined to be a Snowy Owl.

Due, undoubtedly to my owl-like face, Mother breezed past the chapter, "Is your son a werewolf ?" without giving it a thought. But when she came to "Is your son left-handed?" she cried, "Oh, my God," so loudly that I immediately became a candidate for diaper rash.

When Grandmother Area Code 512 rushed in with a Bible in one hand and a fire extinguisher in the other, equally ready to do battle with consensual toe sucking or conflagration, my mother collapsed into tears.

"The shame!" she cried. "The social stigma! I'll never be able to hold my head up in public again!"

"I warned you about marrying that man," Grandmother Area crowed. "Left-handedness is passed on from father to son, just like leprosy and impacted wisdom teeth."

The possibility that I might *not* be left-handed was not considered. That left-handedness existed at all was enough for my mother; that my father existed at all was enough for Grandmother 512.

Sweetheart gave me a sorrowful look and moaned again. Grandmother gently took her hand. "Look at the bright side," she said. "Joan of Arc was left-handed, and so was Queen Victoria."

And Sweetheart wailed, "That's supposed to make me feel *better?* Joan of Arc was burned like a Yule log, and no son of mine is going to be the damn Queen of England!"

But Grandmother Area Code 512's mind had moved on to more important things.

She rested her bony right hand on the side of my crib and raised her left foot.

Anticipating a small fortune from the ticket sales for viewing ex-step Grandfather Billy Area Code 512's suicide, Grandmother had purchased a pair of custom made Tony Lama cowboy-bowling shoes. Replete with little silver bowling pins and little turquoise bowling balls, she looked to be wearing a Christmas tree on each foot. "By grab they were expensive," she admitted, "but I figure it'll take about twenty-two years for that little pecan tree to grow tall enough to hang the little rat, so the money will just keep rolling in!"

The front door slammed and Dung Beetle came in singing, "Heigh-Ho, Heigh-Ho. It's home from work we go…"

Sweetheart flung the book containing the chapter "Is your son left-handed?" at his head, and Dung Beetle, whose normal facial expression is that of mass confusion anyway, ducked too late.

"I didn't carry this child in my belly for nine months just to see him toasted like a left-handed Joan of Arc!" she exclaimed.

"What in the world are you talking about?" he cried. "If Harry is Joan of Arc, then I'm Queen Victoria!"

"I'll tell you what you are," Sweetheart screamed, "you are a left-handed son of a dung beetle bitch!"

Grandmother Area Code 512 did a few steps of a bowling shoe soft-shoe, dropped her shoulder, and hurled an imaginary twelve-pound ball directly at the chiffonier. "Strike!" she cried. "I'll show these Yankees how a Texas girl bowls," she promised.

I could only shake my head in disbelief. I had put it off too long. One way or another I had to find my way back to The Old Home Place.

Later, I put my question point blank to Wyatt.

"Wyatt," I insisted, "where exactly is The Old Home Place? I've got to get out of here. These people are *crazy!*"

The usually straightforward Wyatt dissembled. He wasn't quite sure. He not so subtly segued to the nutritional value of nuts.

"Protein!" he protested. "Most of us don't seem to realize just how important protein is to our bodies." Without a pause for breath he began extolling the jellies and fruit preserves of Provence. From the delicacies of the south of France, Wyatt bounced to Swiss chard, which he quickly rejected with a sour-owl grimace.

"Ding Bling it, Wyatt," I said, "I'm serious. If you don't stop pussy-footing around and tell me where The Old Home Place is, I will soil myself and scream 'brassiere brassiere' as loud as I can."

"OK," Wyatt grumbled, "I'll tell you the truth. One dark night—about ten months ago— Shy Clayton, Metcalf and I were sitting out there on a tree limb minding our own business. Metcalf was a little bleary-eyed because he had been nipping on some stump water. Then, he noticed the light on top of the water tower.

"'Holy cow!' he shouted, 'Jus looka dat star!' ... All right, I'll admit it, maybe Shy Clayton and I had had a little stump water ourselves. Anyway that thing did *look* like star—maybe even two stars.

"So, straight away, the three of us (Shy Clayton, Metcalf and yours truly) took off through the woods to search for some gold, myrrh and frankincense.

"Don't ask me why, maybe it's racial memory, but anytime three Wise Men see a bright star (or even the light on top of a water tower, I guess) they have an irresistible urge to go tromping through the woods after junk like that—baby gifts, you know?

"Now, I'll tell you, Harry, that doggoned frankincense doesn't grow on trees. We looked and looked. Damned frankincense! I don't know why Wise Men even bother with it!"

"Just hold on here, Wyatt. I think I've heard this story. Is this the one with the cows and the sheep and the camel shepherds lying in a manger?"

"Nope," Wyatt promised, "this is a different story entirely. I'm getting to your Old Home Place.

"The first time I laid eyes on you, Shy Clayton, Metcalf and I were peeping through a window. You were lying on the kitchen table screaming, 'Keep that damned octopus away from me!' and, 'Be careful with those scissors!'

"As I told you before, my Old Home Place was an egg, and I hope I never see it again. If *this* isn't your Old Home Place, I just don't know. Maybe you'd better ask your mother."

It didn't seem right. Instinctively I seemed to know that a boy should not ask his mother to show him The Old Home Place. I had seen Dung Beetle's Old Home Place from the window of the "car car."

Grandmother Area Code 512 talked incessantly about her Old Home Place: "In that part of Texas there weren't any trees, so we couldn't have a log house. There wasn't any good sod, so we couldn't have a sod house. All we had was dust, and plenty of it. So pappy built us a dust house, and that's where I was born. I was scarce out of the womb before a little puff of wind blew that place all the way to Lubbock. But, Son, I do miss it."

Everybody talked about *their* Old Home Place, but no one said word about *my* Old Home Place.

I will modestly admit that I believe my self a little brighter than the average, run of the mill owl-faced boy, so I do not know why it took me so long to figure it out. It was *Sweetheart's Secret*; my own mother's guilty, shameful secret! She was harboring an octopus in my Old Home Place! Either through guilt or a misguided sense of compassion (never pity an octopus), she had chosen to push me out and keep my sister, Violet, the bitch octopus.

I lay there, my ego bruised, my sense of self worth in tatters. From the living room came the heartrending tones of Grandmother's guitar as she desecrated Stephen Foster's "Home Sweet Home."

> "There's no place like home,
> Oh, there's no-ho place like home,
> With a cross-eyed baby a sit-ting on your knee,
> There's no-ho place like home."

28

Having arrived at my ten-month birthday, I looked back on what I like to call my "undergraduate days" with a feeling of pride. I had learned much about the ways of humans.

I had honed my various skills to an edge that would turn cutlery makers from Sheffield to Solingen green with envy, and I'm sure my innate abilities in the field of language would be considered astounding—perhaps miraculous—if anyone else were smart enough to understand me.

My natural charm served me in such a manner that I was, even with my owl-like face, accepted by the general public as a fine fellow to be around.

I am wise enough to not take complete credit for my success in life. I arrived in this world with a dedicated support group already in place. There was my family, of course. But I also had Wyatt, my godfather and mentor, and my two god owlcles, Shy Clayton and Metcalf.

Although not actually born with a silver spoon in my mouth, I did receive a silver *plated* spoon soon after my birth.

Even though I seem to have been predestined toward owlism (and mind you, I'm not complaining) I sometimes feel I might have been better suited had I been born to the amphibian persuasion. I am most comfortable in the swamp-like environment that my bladder so willingly provides. I take no offense at the fond nickname Wyatt has given me: "Old Soggy Butt."

Though I say it as one who probably should not, I find satisfaction in my mastery of the art of spit-uppery. So far had I advanced in fact, that Wyatt suggested it was time for me to begin work on projectile vomiting. Of course, with the refined sensibility so evident in owls, he called it regurgitation. It is, Wyatt claims, important for the digestion of food. To my way of thinking: puke is puke, and if owls are too fine to admit it, perhaps they should change their diet.

I suppose I should try to not be so bitchy.

Having come to the conclusion that I was a left-handed, as well as being a somewhat owl-faced boy, Sweetheart began worrying about my emotional stability. She feared the development of an inferiority complex. The reality is quite the opposite, though perhaps Wyatt is the only one who realizes it. In truth, I'm probably the most ferior fellow you will ever meet.

Although Mother immediately labeled my projectile vomiting, or "hurling" if you will, to be another sign of a disturbed child, I determined to give it my very best effort. Indeed, if I do have a fault, it is my insistence on personal perfection.

As I think back on this period of my life I will admit I was considered a "good" baby, a typical human understatement in my opinion. I was an *excellent* baby. I rarely cried or fussed, showing my displeasure only by screaming, "Brassiere brassiere!"

The only really unpleasant part of my life at this time, the excruciating pain, the thorn in my heart, was the lack of progress in returning to The Old Home Place. I remembered that place as being, at the best, "cozy." In point of fact, given my rapidly increasing size, I feared there would not even be room for me to pick my nose. A "small problem," you may say, but can you honestly say that you have gone your whole life without picking your nose? Of course not.

And what about Sweet Little Girl? Surely she was growing as fast as I. If, as was my fondest hope, she joined me when I returned to the womb, she would want to bring her portmanteau. She would need a chiffarobe...and we can't just sit through all eternity staring at one another.

I planned to sing sweet love songs to her, of course, but for that I'd need a lute. Lord, I can only hope that when Mother Nature designed Woman she had the foresight to provide a place in the womb for lute storage.

In truth my ten-month birthday brought me much to look back on, but little to look forward to—except worry. There was, of course, no celebration, no gifts. Even Wyatt had long since stopped bringing me little furry tidbits from the fields. "A fat mouse for Harry is just a waste of a good mouse," he grumbled to Metcalf.

Still in all, when I closed my eyes that night I was a happy boy. I had promised myself to perfect my projectile vomiting until—until my sister Violet stepped out the door of the Old Home Place, and I could get behind her and splat her right on her fat octopus butt.

29

Less than a week after my ten-month birthday I was awakened in the night from a deep sleep. The house rattled as the front door slammed. Dung Beetle screamed for help and Grandmother 512 raced past my door and down the hall toward the living room, a Bible in one hand and a fire extinguisher in the other. The soft, felt spurs on her Tony Lama bedroom slippers neither jingled nor jangled, but produced only a soft, embarrassed, apologetic, "whuth, whuth."

Grandmother later admitted to me she could tell immediately the Bible would be of no help, but she was almost sure she smelled a whiff of "Dung Beetle smoke." So instead of cursing her, he should have been grateful she hosed him down with the fire extinguisher. Though the sticky white liquid proved unnecessary, and did not produce an appreciable amount of gratitude, it *did* slow him down to the point he could explain his terror.

"I've been swooped by a giant goddamn owl!" he cried.

Zagging inadvertently against the étagère, Dung Beetle sent what Mother called a ceramic turkey from the Ming Dynasty (though what Father called a piece of "night-soil") crashing to the floor.

"It was a goddamn foreign owl with slanty eyes, and he swooped me! He was after my passport! My own goddamn American passport. That's what they always want. Damn foreigners." Dung Beetle fought to a draw with the forces of verticality.

Finally, Sweetheart sluggished and shuffled her way past my door crying, "Wha? Wha?"

"Pour your drunken husband into bed," Grandmother disgusted at her. "He claims some Korean owl tried to steal his pisspot!"

Sweetheart shook her head in disbelief. "Let's just all get back to bed," she pleaded.

When I woke again it was morning and Grandmother Area Code 512 sat rocking beside my crib. With her tongue clamped securely between her front teeth, she thumbed with frightening determination through the pages of her Bible concordance. Running her trigger finger down the page, she cackled gutturally at every discovery of "drunkenness" cited.

"Why bless me," Grandmother prouded, "I have enough material here to recriminate your drunken father for the rest of his life!"

And then, with a timing that suggested my life might be choreographed, as Grandmother Area Code left the room, Wyatt, Shy Clayton and Metcalf flew in through the closed window. The very owls I wanted to see!

They each greeted me with a chipper, "Good morning," which I chose to ignore.

I got right to the point. "Ok, you guys, line up. Which of you is responsible for the swooping of my Dung Beetle and the attempted theft of his passport and/or his pisspot?"

Not an eye blinked, although Shy Clayton giggled softly behind the tip of his wing.

"Are you grilling us?" he asked. "I must caution you, grilled owl is tough and stringy and tastes simply awful."

"Your feeble attempt at humor is quite out of place," I assured him, allowing no smile on my "Chief Inspector's" face.

"It couldn't have been one of us, officer," Metcalf chuckled. "We were all in the back seat, singing. My thought is that it was likely a North Korean owl. I understand they are so poor they don't have a passport, nor a window to throw it out of."

Wyatt winced. "Metcalf, for goodness sakes, I'm busting my tail feathers trying to teach young Harry a few linguistic syntaxes here. Please be so good as to not end your sentence with a preposition." An unchastened Metcalf rephrased: "They have neither a window nor that-which-one-might-reasonably-expect a passport from-it-to-be-thrown. Does that suit you, your Royal Professorship?"

Wyatt mumbled a quiet, "I'm really not sure."

"Boys," I sighed, "no more Dung Beetle swooping. It simply causes too much disruption. Grandmother 512 is planning to seek legal restitution to pay for having her fire extinguisher recharged, and divine retribution against Dung Beetle for alienation of affection to her nervous system."

A still-miffed Metcalf goosed the pedantic Wyatt as he took his leave through the window.

The morning sun found Dung Beetle resting his head on his elbow and proclaiming the worst case of amnesia he'd ever had. To the best of his memory, he said, he had never, ever, seen a North Korean owl in this neighborhood—and Grandmother was full of you-know-what.

The dutiful, though gleeful, Grandmother Area Code 512, rocked beside his bed, Bible in hand, her very presence guaranteeing that a quick death for him would be a welcome one.

Sweetheart, phone in hand, was loudly disputing the insurance agent's assertion that Ming Dynasty night soil/ceramic turkeys, accidentally smithereened by a man who had been swooped by a North Korean owl, were not covered by her current policy.

I held my hands tightly over my ears and prayed to be returned to The Old Home Place, even if it meant living with an octopus.

30

Pumpkin, who now insists on being called "Lilith," threatened to do unspeakable things to parts of my body I didn't even know I had, if I failed to address her as she wished.

When this so-called "Lilith" was distracted for a moment, I slipped my hand down and checked. She was right! I had it, or them. Strange, indeed, that this seemingly useless appendage had not been scissored away at my birth when the "trimming Harry" craze seemed to be all the rage. From the feel of it, they should have rattled when I shook the bag, but no sound was emitted. As with my eyebrows, this unplayable little package was evidently placed there for purely ornamental reasons. And as with Sweetheart's lately lamented Ming Dynasty night soil/ceramic turkey, it appeared to be just one more thing to dust.

Her attention once more focused on me as she continued her tirade: "I am not a pumpkin! A pumpkin is a fruit, do I look like a fruit to you? I am Lilith. I am a woman.

I know—I could have corrected her and told her she was a baby, but somehow the time just didn't seem right.

"Then Pumpk…, that is…*Lilith*, does that mean you manifest all the wisdom and strength, as well as, obviously, the beauty of all women?"

"Even as you, a potential man, represent idiocy."

"And could you, in your wisdom," I tried to keep my sly grin on the inside of my face, "conceivably tell me just where my Old Home Place is?"

"Conceive, in any of its forms, is not a word I care to hear, but, yes, I could."

"And will you?"

"I will not!"

"Well, dog poop!" I cried in frustration, "Why not?"

"You forget, I'm privy to your plan to evict your poor sister, Violet, from her home. Violet is a female, and therefore one of mine."

"Violet is a goddamn octopus," I sort of screamed. "I am your own kind, a human!"

"Maybe yes. Maybe no. The word on the street is that you are not really committed. You may yet embrace the owl persuasion. Boy oh boy, will you be tickled when you have feathers at your groin!"

"Lilith, you may be a woman, but Henny Youngman you ain't. That joke was graffiti carved on Stonehenge. It wasn't funny then and it's not funny now."

Fast as lightning she lunged for my heretofore-unknown little package. But good old yours truly was just a tad bit faster; I flipped to my belly.

"Shit!" she cried, grabbing a handful of my diaper.

"Night soil," I replied with a smile. "We call it night soil."

Once again the knowledge for which I have so fervently searched, the veritable Holy Grail of knowledge, had been denied me. There was no use appealing again to Wyatt, he would just tell me to ask my mother. Yeah. Sure. As the French would say, "It is to laugh." About as funny as having groin feathers.

31

As I grew older, I found my mind becoming conflicted. I asked myself: Who am I? Why am I here? What is my purpose in life?

Mother, aka Sweetheart, was obviously placed in this human world to feed me, to comfort me and to force me to drink eight bottles of water every day. Father, aka Dung Beetle, seemed to mostly…I guess, just be Dung Beetle. That, of course, included amusing me by constantly badgering and annoying Grandmother Area Code 512. And there could be no more diligent, more persistent, more dedicated Grandmother-annoyer in all the world than he.

Grandmother Area Code 512 also has an "aka," although she does not know it. It was a gift from Dung Beetle who shared it only with me, because if Grandmother ever heard it she would rupture his spleen. I am sworn to secrecy.

Why was a grandmother living in our house? I do not know. Neither Sweet Little Girl nor Pumpkin-cum-Lilith had such a thing. Dung Beetle's theory is that, like the appendix, the "grandmother" is a useless appendage whose original use has been lost in the mists of time.

I flattered myself in feeling that I had a clearer picture of the broad view than he.

I knew Grandmother also had been provided to amuse me. If we consider "annoyance" as a Ping-Pong game between the two of them, Grandmother never failed to return his serves, and sometimes she beat the pants off him.

A Grandmother can also remove her teeth…all of them. Was that meant to be a gift from God to me? Surely it was all the proof I needed that He loves me. In fact, how could I doubt that He was involved in what seemed to be some master plan to keep me happy?

But there was something fishy. The clouds of doubt and suspicion began to hover at the edges of my mind. Could it really be that this vast coming together of such disparate beings was for the benefit of *me*, Harry, the owl-faced boy? Or was it a devious and sinister plot, with my happiness only secondary to the real intent?

An epiphany, please!

And the winner is…yes!…my sister, Violet, the bitch octopus!

I see it now. Keep dumb old Harry laughing. Take him for rides in the "car car." Aye, give the lad the occasional dram of cold beer, *anything* to take his mind off The Old Home Place where Violet cavorts and frolics in regal splendor!

Evil, thy name is Violet!

Yet, World, grant me one wish before I so willingly exit this life and join the multitude of unwanted owl-faced boys. Let not my Sweet Little Girl be a part of this scam.

"Holy cow, Harry," Wyatt exclaimed as he settled himself on the footboard of my crib. "Why so glum? You have the look of an aggrieved, put-upon, oh-lord-why-me angst-ridden teenager."

"And well I might! I've just had a most unwelcome Epiphany. And, compared to the way we usually think of epiphanies, this was a piss-poor one."

"Now, come, come, my boy. It can't be so bad as to warrant a capital E."

"But I've just learned that the happiness in my life has been only a pawn to distract me from thinking about The Old Home Place!"

Metcalf flew in through the closed window, landed beside Wyatt on the footboard, and adjusted himself to a comfortable position.

"Did I hear someone mention prawns?" He asked. "I love prawns."

"The word is 'pawn.'" Wyatt advised. "It comes from Late Latin, and it means 'One who has broad feet.' Would you say that your happiness has broad feet, Harry?"

"Boy, about a half dozen succulent prawns would set pretty well in my old belly right now," Metcalf mused.

Shy Clayton swooshed in next. "Say, fellows, I've been wondering. If an owl were to be crossed with an octopus, would the resultant issue have eight feathery groins?"

Holy cow.

If we acknowledge that a group of lions is called a "pride," and a group of geese is called a "gaggle," could we not, *please*, call these three owls a "hopeless of owls"?

32

Life, by definition, goes on. And, as the weeks and months passed toward the end of my first year, the devastating wound caused by the conspirators standing between The Old Home Place and me healed slowly—and only somewhat.

Despite my best efforts at self-pity, I still found things that made me laugh. Sweetheart's tummy seemed to get larger everyday, and my fertile mind was kept busy thinking up new, "Yo mama is *so* fat," jokes.

And, Lord help us, Dung Beetle had started growing a mustache! Constantly turning himself this way and that, admiring himself before the mirror, he'd ask, "See anything different about me, Harry?"

"You have one green eye and one brown eye," I replied. "That's different."

"No, I mean something really different."

"Oh yes," I told him, "you have a smudge of dirt on your upper lip."

He smiled a forced smile. "That, my unobservant son, is hair. It will soon be a fine, luxuriant mustache."

"Father, with all due respect, I have more hair on my derrière than you have on your face."

"Not so!" he cried. And with that he removed the mirror from the wall to facilitate a comparison. I unpinned my diaper and flipped to my tummy.

It was then that Grandmother Area Code 512, Bible in hand, stepped into the room to read me my daily scripture. The mirror showed her two huge smiles: one, on my dimpled tush, the other on Dung Beetle's face. "My Lord, what now?" she screamed, and fainted dead away.

Later, Wyatt explained Mother's swelling tummy. He did not even try to explain Dung Beetle's mustache. "Pregnant," he announced. "Your mother is pregnant."

"And so? I've heard of a pregnant moment, and I've heard of a pregnant pause, but what is a pregnant Sweetheart?"

"A pregnant Sweetheart is bad news, Harry. B-a-d n-e-w-s. It means that in a few months you will have a new brother or sister."

"I shan't!" I cried. "I refuse! I'll not have some snot-nosed kid running around slobbering on my steak tartar!"

"But, Harry," Wyatt reminded, "you don't eat steak tartar."

"Well, not after someone possibly named "Eugene" or, maybe, "Lucile" has slobbered on it, I don't!"

I wept. I screamed, but to no avail. At length, finding me inconsolable, Wyatt bade me goodnight and took his leave.

Sweetheart came with a bottle of water. "I know your problem, little Harry Warry. You are lonely. But soon you will be blessed with a little brother or sister. Won't that be nice?"

Suddenly I realized what my "blessing" would be. My blessing would be a goddamned octopus with red toenails.

Still, on thinking about it, I took some comfort in knowing that at last Violet was being evicted.

In fact, there might be a small glimmer of hope. Without a doubt, The Old Home Place was growing larger every day. Without Violet there would be room aplenty, room for Sweet Little Girl's portmanteau, her chiffarobe. With luck I might find a shelf on which I could keep a lute, and sheet music for "Flow Gently Sweet Afton" and "The Lonely Ash Grove."

By Wyatt's reckoning I had already passed the point of no return as far as becoming an owl; I would remain a human boy for all eternity.

I resigned myself to that fate with surprising ease. But the thought that I could now return to The Old Home Place left me giddy.

I must admit my mind soared with extravagant ideas. At the rate The Old Home Place was expanding, there could, perhaps, be room for me to erect a basketball goal. And during those times when I wasn't playing "Flow Gently Sweet Afton" on the lute, I could shoot a few baskets.

At last, as it inevitably must, the big day arrived. Dawn came, and with it a baby sister. And yes, it is Violet, but not *the* Violet.

With my first, brief glimpse I was delighted to see that she has no tentacles. She was blessed with the usual human arms and legs. As to whether or not she has feathers at the groin, I have been unable to ascertain.

Mother, aka Sweetheart, rocks the new child. And mother is soft, smiling, as mothers tend to be.

Father, aka Dung Beetle, seems to equate both his mustache and his new child as a validation of his superior manhood.

Grandmother Area Code 512 hovers nearby singing the Doxology in what she believes to be the key of D.

There is talk of soon celebrating my first birthday.

Wyatt and the god owlcles are flying through the neighborhood passing out White Owl cigars.

And yours truly? Why, I'm packing— and wondering about the best way to move a chiffarobe.

About the Author

Max Yoho has established himself as a witty writer from the nation's Heartland. He has published award winning novels, poetry, short stories and essays. A growing list of fans enjoy his off-beat sense of humor and mind boggling leaps of logic—leaving readers laughing out loud.

Max is a lifelong Kansan. Born in 1934, he lived in Colony until he was ten. His next home was Atchison, then Topeka, where he graduated from Topeka High School and attended Washburn University.

He worked 38 years as a machinist. After retiring in 1992, Max developed what had started as a short story into his first novel, *The Revival*. Published in 2001, the novel won the 2002 J. Donald Coffin Memorial Book Award of Kansas Authors Club. A second novel, *Tales from Comanche County*, grew from Max's memories of his great aunt and great uncle. Max's poems, essays and short stories are collected in *Felicia, These Fish Are Delicious*. *The Moon Butter Route*, a novel about bootlegging in Southeastern Kansas, was among the first books listed as Kansas Notable Books by the Kansas Center for the Book. This book also won the 2007 J. Donald Coffin Memorial Book Award of Kansas Authors Club.

In *With the Wisdom of Owls* Max shares truths from his "deep memory." Readers familiar with Max's writing will recognize this work as dippings from Max's deep well of mirth and humor, reflecting his "slanch-wise" view of everyday life.

www.ingramcontent.com/pod-product-compliance
Lightning Source LLC
Chambersburg PA
CBHW051254170626
46809CB00004B/1644